Family Pose
(Hughes)

FAMILY POSE

Books by Dean Hughes

NUTTY FOR PRESIDENT
HONESTLY, MYRON
SWITCHING TRACKS
MILLIE WILLENHEIMER AND THE
CHESTNUT CORPORATION
NUTTY AND THE CASE OF THE
MASTERMIND THIEF
NUTTY AND THE CASE OF THE
SKI-SLOPE SPY
JELLY'S CIRCUS
NUTTY CAN'T MISS
THEO ZEPHYR
NUTTY KNOWS ALL
FAMILY POSE

FAMILY POSE

Dean Hughes

New York
ATHENEUM

Atheneum
Macmillan Publishing Company
866 Third Avenue, New York, NY 10022
Collier Macmillan Canada, Inc.

Printed in the United States of America
10 9 8 7 6 5 4

Library of Congress Cataloging-in-Publication Data
Hughes, Dean,
Family pose.
Summary: Feeling unwanted, an eleven-year-old orphan
runs away from his foster home and lives on the streets
until he finds a new type of family at a hotel.
[1. Runaways—Fiction. 2. Homeless persons—Fiction.
3. Orphans—Fiction] I. Title.
PZ7.H87312Fam 1989 [Fic] 88-28501
ISBN 0-689-31396-9

For Gordon and Sharon Allred

FAMILY POSE

1

David liked the warmth, the comfort. He even liked the vibrations coming from the old Coke machine. For a minute or two he resisted sleep and clung to the pleasure. But he was soon drifting, hearing the unsteady buzz and feeling the touch of the soft towel along the side of his face. He knew that someone might find him here, but it didn't matter; he was now beyond caring.

Later, when he heard the sound, the voice, he knew he was actually hearing it for the third time, and he knew that time had passed, that he had been asleep for an hour or two.

"Come on. Get up."

The man sounded angry. David was so tired, so groggy, that he was not thinking clearly. All the same, the fear was back, grabbing at his stomach, shaking him awake. David pushed back the towels and stood up. He wondered what the man would do.

"You're going to have to . . ." He stopped, and David looked up at him for the first time. The guy swore and then shook his head. "You're just a kid."

David didn't speak. He was too scared.

"What are you doing in here?"

David looked down, away from the man's eyes. He wondered about the clothes the man was wearing: a gold-colored coat and a bow tie. David thought he must be a bellboy, but he wasn't sure; he had never really been in a hotel before.

"How did you get up here without anyone seeing you?"

David was not about to tell him, but it didn't take much to figure it out. He had waited and watched until no one was in the lobby, and he had hurried to the elevator while the man at the hotel desk was looking in another direction. He had pushed the seventh-floor button, for no particular reason, and once on the floor had discovered the corner where the Coke machine was—a little room without a door—and had found towels on a maid's cart, enough to make a bed.

"Did you run away from home or something?"

David stared at the buttons on the gold coat, and he waited. Something told him it was better to say nothing, not even to try any explanations. The anger seemed gone from the man's voice, but David knew better than to trust him. Adults always tried to get his trust—but sooner or later they used it against him.

The man cursed again, but softly. "Look, you can't come in here and sleep. I can't let you do that." He hesitated and seemed to consider. "Why don't you just tell me who you are and I'll call your folks. They're probably worried sick about you. Is that what's going on? Did you get in a fight with your old man and take off?"

David didn't need this. "I'll go now. Just let me go, okay?" He took a step.

"Wait a minute." The man didn't move, but he didn't know what to do; David could see that. He was not an old guy. He was maybe forty or so. But there was something old-fashioned about him. His hair was black and slicked down, like guys in old movies. He was sort of handsome, too, like the stars in those films. "You've been on the street a few days, haven't you? I'll bet you're hungry."

That was true. David had been scrounging food as best he could, spending his money carefully. But he couldn't ask for food. He wasn't going to do that. He just needed to get away, get outside again, do things for himself.

"Look, kid, you're not giving me any choice. You better give me a number to call. You don't want to spend any more nights on the street, do you? It's cold out there."

"Just let me go, okay? I won't come back here again."

The man shook his head. "I don't know what I ought to do. You aren't a street kid. I can see how scared you are. I think maybe I better call the police. They'll figure out where you're from and take you home."

"Just let me go." Above all, David didn't want police. He never wanted to look at Mr. Poulter again, didn't want to hear the things he would say.

The man still refused to move, and he was blocking the way. He kept staring down at David. "Look," he finally said, "come with me. I don't know what else to do." He

3

turned, and as he did, he took hold of David's arm. David was surprised, and he pulled back, cringing.

"Hey, I'm not going to hurt you. But that's what you expect, isn't it? I'll bet your old man pounds on you."

That wasn't true. But it didn't matter.

"Look, this just might be the stupidest thing I've ever done, but I'm going to open up a room for you, and I'm going to let you sleep in there for the night. I don't want to put you out on the street, and I hate to call the cops. But in the morning you better tell me where you live. I can probably even get you a ride home." He turned and walked down the hall, this time not holding David's arm. David followed, even though he knew he had to be careful. He told himself he wouldn't stay all night. He would sneak out before morning. But at least he could sleep for a while and be warm.

The man pulled a set of keys from his pocket and opened a door. Then he reached inside and flipped the light on. David stepped in behind him. The room was nice, not big, but pretty, and filled with a clean smell, like the hand soap his mother had always used. David had never slept a single night of his life in a place this fancy.

"You're going to have to sleep on the floor. I'll find you some blankets and a . . . no, go ahead and sleep in the bed. I'll get a maid to fix it up. Do you want something to eat now, or do you want to wait until morning?"

David wanted something now. But he didn't want to say. He took his coat off and set it on a chair.

"Are you hungry?"

"No."

4

The man laughed, softly. "You wouldn't make much of an actor." He walked over and checked the thermostat on the wall. "I'll turn the heat up a little. You're shivering."

David hadn't known that. He hadn't thought of being cold. But he liked the idea of the room being warm.

"The dining room is closed now, but there's an all-night hamburger place across the street. I'll go over there and get you something. I just don't know whether you can stay awake that long. Can you?"

David nodded.

The man smiled. He had straight white teeth, like those old movie stars. "You're hungry, all right," he said. He walked to the door and stopped. "My name's Paul. I'm the night bellboy—or at least I am tonight. If I get caught hiding you in here, I'll get my butt kicked clear out of this place. You can't leave this room or make any noise, okay?"

David nodded again.

"You got a name?"

David looked away.

"Hey, what's that going to hurt? Just tell me your first name."

But David knew he couldn't do that. He knew better than to open up to this man—he had made that mistake before.

"You know, I didn't have to let you in here."

David heard the tone, the hint of anger. The guy was like all the rest. He didn't give without expecting something. He probably wanted a name so he could turn David in. "I'll leave. That's okay."

5

Paul shook his head and swore. He looked disgusted. "Is that all you know how to say?"

David grabbed his coat. He should have known better in the first place. He was getting out.

But Paul stood between David and the door. "Hey, never mind," he said. "I don't need to know your name. I'll be back in a few minutes. I'll get you something to eat. You get undressed and get in bed." He went out and shut the door.

David wondered. Maybe he should take off now, while he had a chance. But he wanted that bed, the clean smell, and he wanted the food. He kicked off his shoes without unlacing them, pulled his T-shirt over his head and tossed it on a chair, and dropped his jeans to the floor. All the while he was looking at the TV, trying to see how it turned on. He stepped out of his jeans, turned the volume knob down, and then pushed the power button. He began twisting another knob, changing channels until he found a movie channel, and then he got in bed. The big bed had sheets that were smooth, almost stiff, and the bedspread was slick, like silk. He put both pillows behind him and sat up. He had never had a TV in his room before. But every day, after school, he had gone straight home and watched the afternoon movies. Of course, that was before everything had happened.

David felt out of place in this room, but he liked it. The bed was big, with a little table and lamp on each side. There were a couple of big chairs with flowered upholstery that matched the bedspread, and a fancy mirror hanging over an old-fashioned chest of drawers.

David slipped back out of bed and went to use the bathroom. The tile, black and white in patterns, was cold through his socks, and the sink, with a gold faucet, looked very old. But all was shiny. He could smell lemon and the other smell—a sweet sort of soap. He washed his face and hands, one of the few times ever without being told, and he felt a little better. He told himself he would take a shower in the morning or sit in the bathtub, all filled up. And then he would leave—early, before Paul came back and started asking more questions.

He got back in bed and tried to wait. But a strange coldness was in his chest. He was scared—scared to be alone, scared Paul might be downstairs calling the police, still scared from all he had been through the last few days. The only feeling as powerful was the overwhelming tiredness that quivered through his muscles, his mind. He was asleep in just a few minutes, and when he heard Paul's voice next to the bed, he was startled all over again. He struggled for a moment to think where he was.

"Look, kid, I don't know which you need more, food or sleep, but here's a hamburger and some fries." Paul set the tray down on one of the nightstands. He had a strange, smooth way of moving, as though he were gliding, not really walking.

"What've you got on television?"

David shrugged.

"You're like me. I don't like to be alone that much. I turn on the TV and then I don't watch it. But I like to have somebody talking, or music going—or something."

David thought he heard a kind of sadness in the man's

voice—something he hadn't noticed before. He wondered what sort of person Paul was. But then he pushed the thought away. It didn't matter; David wouldn't get to know him. He seemed okay, but David had no doubt that he was just like all the rest.

"Go ahead and eat."

David picked up the big hamburger in both hands, and he leaned over the tray. Juice ran over his fingers.

Paul took the paper off a straw and then stuck it through the plastic lid of a drink in a Styrofoam cup. "That's a chocolate shake. Is that okay?"

"Sure."

"I've got to get back down to the floor now. Do you want to leave this TV on?"

David nodded.

"Okay, but keep it low, like it is. It'll give you some light in the room, too. Are you scared to be alone?"

"No."

"You wouldn't say if you were, would you?"

David kept eating. It was the most food he had had at one time in two days.

Paul walked to the door. He stopped and stood there for a few seconds, and then he walked back to the foot of the bed. "You really need to go back home, you know."

"I'll leave in the morning," David said.

Paul blew his breath out slowly. "Leave and go where?"

David went back to eating.

"How old are you anyway?"

"Fourteen."

"I think you're ten."

"Twelve." That was almost true. David was eleven, almost twelve. But he was small for his age.

Paul stood with his hands on his hips, his jacket bulging over his wrists. "Look, maybe we can figure something out in the morning."

David nodded, but only to end the conversation. He would leave early. He would sleep for a while, and then he would sneak out.

Paul walked to the door again. "Okay. Remember. Don't leave the room. If you need someone, call me—four two four two. But don't get mixed up and call some other number. Remember, four two four two. Just stay right here in the morning. I work all night, and I'll bring you some breakfast after I get off at seven. We'll have to get you out of here not long after that, so finish up that hamburger and then get to sleep." Paul turned the light switch, leaving only the flickering light from the television set. "You can turn that lamp on, if you want."

"Okay." But David didn't turn it on.

"You sure you're not scared?"

"Yeah. I'm okay."

"Right." Paul laughed, almost silently.

As Paul went out the door David said, "Thanks," but not so Paul could have heard it. In a few seconds he was asleep again, his hamburger only half-eaten.

2

David was still sound asleep when Paul came into the room the next morning. It was a Friday morning, an overcast November day, even a little foggy. The room was still dark except for the shadowy light from the television set. David was surprised it was morning. He had planned to be gone by now.

Paul was holding a tray covered with a green cloth. "I don't think you moved all night," he said. "I checked on you a couple of times. You were sleeping like a log. Are you still tired?"

David nodded. He was more than tired. He could hardly think through the haze that was clinging to his mind.

Paul walked to the little bed stand, picked up last night's tray, and set down the new one. "You didn't even stay awake long enough to finish your food," he said.

David noticed the smoothness again. Paul's steps never

seemed to strike the floor, and he shifted the tray from his hand onto the table with the same kind of motion, like a waiter at a fancy restaurant. David had seen guys like that in the movies. Paul's voice had a certain smoothness, too, soft and sort of gentle, and yet a little practiced, as though he tried to sound that way. It was that voice that David didn't trust. The other voice, the one filled with sadness, was gone now.

"Listen . . . why don't you eat and then sleep some more?"

"No. I've got to go." David threw back the covers and pushed his legs over the side of the bed.

"No you don't. There might be something I can do for you. I'm looking into some things. You might as well stick around for a little while."

That was the last thing David wanted—Paul meddling in his life. He had been through enough of that. But he kept sitting where he was—still so tired that getting up seemed impossible.

"Look, I've got to be back here by three this afternoon and work my regular shift—I was just filling in for a guy last night. So I've got to get home and get some sleep. But I'm going to make some phone calls this afternoon and see—"

David's head jerked around.

"Hey, I'm not calling the cops—don't worry. But there's a kid named Arnie who used to work here while he was in college. He's a social worker now. He knows all about this kind of stuff. I think he can figure something out for you."

"No he can't." David slipped off the bed and stood up.

"You don't know that. I'll talk to him and see what he has to say. If you're in some kind of messed-up home, he can maybe find you a better place to live. That's gotta be better than wandering around in the streets."

David picked up his jeans and started pulling them on.

"Hey, wait a second. Don't be stupid. I told you I'm not turning you in. Let's just see what this guy has to say. What can that hurt?"

David grabbed his shirt. He was leaving.

"Okay, fine. If you want to take off, go ahead. I don't know what difference it should make to me. But you're not very smart if you pass up a chance to rest up today and stay warm. And you're just plain stupid if you won't even try to work something out." Paul didn't wait to see what David would do; he walked out and shut the door behind him.

David was mad. Paul didn't know what he was talking about. He had no idea how long David had tried to "work things out." And yet, David wondered why Paul cared either way, why he would bother to get involved. It was not that, however, that kept David there; it was the thought of sleeping some more in that nice bed, of staying warm a little while longer. He ate the breakfast, and then he slipped back into bed, not bothering to take his clothes off again. He would only sleep for an hour or two. Then he would go.

The next time David woke, someone was in the room again. He rolled over and blinked his eyes, and then he sat up, suddenly.

"It's okay, kid." It was a young guy—Hispanic. He was

wearing a white jacket, like a waiter, and he had a tray of food. "Paul told me to bring you lunch. He paid for it, and he told me what was going on. I'm not telling no one." He walked over and set the tray down, but he didn't have Paul's smoothness.

"Take a look at this." He pulled the cloth cover off the tray. David saw a sandwich and potato chips, a glass of milk, and a big piece of cake. "Not bad, huh?"

David nodded. He wasn't really hungry yet. Maybe he could save some of it and take it with him.

"Paul said to tell you not to go nowhere. I'm leaving at three, but he'll be back by then. So just sit tight. Live good, man. Not every day you get to kick back and get waited on."

The guy moved toward the door with a kind of cocky walk, and then he grinned at David once more before he went out. David felt uneasy. He knew he would have to leave soon.

The TV was still on and a movie was playing. Police cars were chasing a guy in a red convertible. David thought he would watch for only a few minutes. But before long he was slipping the pillows behind his back. He ate the potato chips, and then the cake, with the milk, but he saved the sandwich. He would take that with him.

When the movie ended he decided to leave, but he didn't get up. He wondered what would be on next. And when the next movie started, he kept letting himself watch another few minutes. He liked sitting in the bed, with the TV close at hand, and he liked having plenty of food. He went ahead and ate the sandwich.

He finally decided he would watch the rest of this movie and then go for sure. He didn't know what time it was, but he thought he could still be gone before three.

As it turned out, however, Paul showed up earlier than David had expected. He came in and sat down in the chair. He wasn't wearing his uniform. He had on a black shirt and a gray jacket, and his hair was shiny and slick. He looked a little younger, but he also looked like he was trying to be younger than he really was. David hadn't noticed before how thin he was. His cheeks had little flesh on them, and the skin along his neck seemed loose.

Paul sat down on the chair by the door. "Did you get enough to eat?" he asked. He had a way of smiling, nodding, and speaking softly, using his voice like a gentle stroke. David felt comfort in that, and yet he kept telling himself not to believe it. He didn't really trust words anymore, and a nice voice didn't change anything.

David nodded in response. He thought he should thank Paul, and yet, he was embarrassed and still nervous about saying too much.

"Don't worry about the busboy—Alberto. He won't say anything."

David was trying to watch the movie.

"Listen, I tried to get hold of Arnie, but they said he wasn't in the office today. We won't be able to get him until Monday now. But the hotel is really quiet this weekend. I told the desk clerk this room was out of order, and it's flagged that way on the computer—so they won't check anyone in here. You might as well just stick around and stay warm. On Monday, we'll see what Arnie can work out for you."

David looked toward the TV, but he wasn't paying attention to the movie now. He was trying to think what he would do. Why was Paul doing this?

"Maybe—if things are really bad in your house—he can get you into a foster home or something like that. I talked to the woman who answered the phone down there at Social Services, and she said that's what they usually try to do."

David slid off the bed, reached down, and got his shoes. He wasn't interested in any more foster homes. Besides, Paul suddenly sounded like someone trying to sell something. "I'll leave now," David said.

"Hey, don't start that again. What's the good of walking out of here? Think a little bit. Don't you want to work something out?"

"No."

"Why not?"

David tied his shoelaces. Paul wanted him to talk, but he wasn't going to do it.

"Why not? Just tell me that."

David stood up and looked around for his coat.

"Tell me why. Are you afraid they'll send you back home?"

David nodded. It wasn't the truth; it wasn't even close. But it was just as well to let Paul think what he wanted to think. Maybe it would end the conversation.

"Why not give it a shot? If worse comes to worst, you could run away again. Look at it that way." Paul tried to laugh. But David knew what was happening; adults always played the same kind of games. They worked together.

"I'm just going to go." David grabbed his coat from the

floor, near the bed. He pulled it on, but he didn't bother to zip it up. He started for the door.

"Wait a minute." Paul stood up quickly and moved in front of him. "Where are you going? Where are you going to sleep tonight?"

"I'll be okay."

"What's that supposed to mean? You'll freeze your little butt off out there. It's starting to rain."

"Just let me go."

"Okay. Fine." Paul cursed, and David saw the muscles in his temples tighten, saw his eyes squeeze with anger. "You're not my problem. I don't know why I tried to help you out in the first place." David felt the cold return to his chest, felt glad he hadn't talked more, hadn't opened up to this guy. He would get away, and he'd take his chances outside. He tried to get to the door, but Paul didn't move. He pointed a finger at David's face. "You know, I put myself on the line for you. I'll lose my job if anyone finds out I kept you up here last night."

"I didn't ask you for anything."

"Well, you sure took it. You didn't turn down any of the meals I brought up here."

David had no answer for that, but he was not about to apologize. He stared back at Paul, defiantly.

"You know what you're doing, don't you? I thought you were some poor little kid who needed help, but you played me for the sucker. It hasn't even crossed your mind that you just might say 'thanks,' instead of 'I didn't ask you for anything.' "

"Thanks a million," David said, biting off the words.

"Thanks from the bottom of my heart. Now let me go."

Paul pulled a fist from his jacket. "Watch your mouth, kid. Do you hear me? You smart off to me one more time and I'll knock you across this room."

David didn't move, just stared back at Paul. "You must be really tough if you can beat up kids my size."

Suddenly Paul's hand lashed out. He grabbed David's shoulder, dug his fingers in deep. The other fist shook in front of the boy's eyes.

David waited. He almost wished Paul would hit him. He needed the rage. Hatred was so much better than what he had been feeling for so long. He held his ground, held the look of defiance, tried to say, "I hate you," with his eyes. But he was shaking all over, and suddenly he realized that he was on the verge of crying.

Paul stared down at David for a long time, didn't move, but David watched the muscles in his face begin to relax. "You're scared to death," he said. "You're shaking all over." It was a kind of accusation, as though Paul were trying to say, "You're not so tough," but it sounded more like an apology.

"That's what you think," David said. The shaking was in his voice now. That was embarrassing; he tried to save himself by pushing past Paul and grabbing the doorknob.

"Just a second," Paul said. He grabbed David's arm, but not with pressure.

"No. I want to go." David pulled the door open. He walked to the elevator and pushed the button. But when he glanced back at Paul, he was surprised at what he saw. Paul was still standing by the door, but he was leaning with his back against the wall. He had his hands in his pockets, and he was looking down at the red carpet at his feet. David didn't know what it meant.

Some time passed, several seconds. The elevator was moving, slowing down to stop. David felt confused. Paul finally glanced up and the two looked at each other straight on. The elevator stopped humming, clanked, and then the door opened.

"Wait," Paul said.

David was going to step into the elevator, but he didn't. Paul was coming, and the door was shutting.

"I'm sorry," Paul said. There was no smoothness now. "I have a bad temper." He waited for a time, stood close to David but didn't look at him. "I'd feel a lot better about this whole thing if you'd stick around for the weekend."

"Why? You don't have to worry about me."

"It's raining. It's cold outside. I just hate to see you go out in that."

"What difference does it make to you?" David wanted so badly to be angry.

"Let me tell you something. Come here for a second." Paul turned and walked back toward the room. David hesitated until Paul was halfway to the door, but then he followed, even though he knew he shouldn't.

When they got to the room, Paul sat down in the chair again. David went to the bed, was about to sit down, and then decided to stand. He wasn't staying long.

Paul didn't look at David. He looked down at the carpet again. "When I was your age, I was in a bad situation. Maybe something like you're in—I don't know. My dad drank a lot. And he was mean when he drank. One time he grabbed me by the hair and threw me. I hit a door frame and it sliced my head wide open. This scar right here on my forehead came from that. He didn't even get it sewed up because he didn't want to admit to anyone how it happened."

David saw the scar.

"The next morning he was all over me, trying to hug me and kiss me and tell me how sorry he was. I didn't tell him it was all right and he hated me for that, but I didn't care. I just made up my mind I was getting out as soon as I could. The only thing is, I waited until I figured I could handle it. I stuck it out until I was sixteen."

That wouldn't work for David. His situation wasn't the same at all. But he couldn't tell Paul that.

"When I did finally take off, I looked old for my age. It wasn't that hard to find work. But I'll tell you, I went through some bad stuff. And if you think I made it through all right, you're wrong. I messed up just about everything. I thought I was doing okay, but now I look back and I know I haven't had any real life—not the kind a guy ought to have. Do you see what I'm saying?"

David thought so.

"All I'm telling you is that I do know something about what might be going on. I know that things can get bad enough to make a kid like you want to take off. But I also know what it means to do it."

David nodded. He thought Paul did know, and he felt something inside himself give way, even as he was fighting not to let it happen. And yet, Paul didn't understand at all.

He had the wrong idea. David had never been beaten. His real father had gotten drunk sometimes, but that was not the problem.

"Don't leave tonight, okay? Let's try to figure something out. At least stay the weekend."

David was still saying to himself that he had to leave, but he also knew it wasn't true. He had already let go; he was staying.

"I've got to go get my uniform on and clock in. I'll bring you up some supper after a while."

David nodded, and then he said, very softly, "Thanks."

"We'll work something out," Paul said.

David wondered what it could be, wondered if there really was some answer. But he didn't think so. He had thought it all through hundreds of times.

When Paul left, David took off his shoes and his jeans, and he got back in bed. The movie was almost over, and he wasn't sure what had happened. But he didn't think much about it. He was relieved not to be going back out in the cold. It had rained one night before since he had left the Poulters' house, and he hadn't forgotten what a long night it had been. And yet, he knew he was working himself into a trap by sticking around.

Paul came back after a while. He brought a big meal—fish, and rice, and fresh peas. It wasn't stuff David liked very much, but it looked nice, all fancy with cloth napkins and shiny silverware. Paul put it down on the table the way he had the night before, gracefully.

"Were you a waiter once or something?" David asked.

Paul looked surprised. "Uh . . . no. Not exactly. I've been around hotels my whole life. Bellboys always take the drinks to the rooms. We end up serving food some-times, too. It's just something I've picked up."

"How long have you worked here?" David didn't really want to know—but he thought he should say something. He didn't know exactly why.

"I've only been here at the Jefferson the last year or so. But I went to San Francisco when I was still just a kid—not long after I left home. That's where I've been most of my life. I worked in the best hotels down there. I was at the St. Francis for a long time. That's about the classiest hotel in San Francisco."

"How come you moved up here?"

"It's kind of a long story. I grew up in Renton, just south of here. My mother still lives down there. She's getting old."

David nodded again. He couldn't think of anything else to say.

"Look, I've got to get back to the floor. Do you mind telling me your first name?"

He wasn't going to say it, and then he did. "David."

"Okay." The two looked at each other for a moment. David felt embarrassed. And maybe Paul did, too.

"I get off at eleven tonight. I might look in sometime before then. But you better get to sleep fairly early. I won't bother you later on. There's a guy who works the night shift on the front desk. His name is Rob. I better tell him what's going on. He's an okay guy, and I can tell him why the room is flagged and he won't say anything. But if you need something, or you get scared, you could call him. Just dial two one one one and he'll answer."

"Okay."

"All right. I'm not on shift until three tomorrow, but I'll come by in the morning, or else call you."

"Okay."

"I . . ." Paul hesitated, searching for words, but then he only said, "Well, I'll talk to you tomorrow."

David nodded. But he was a little frightened. He really didn't want to like this man. He had made enough mistakes already.

3

David didn't eat much. He wasn't that hungry. Before long he fell asleep. He had slept very little in the last few days, and now his body wanted nothing more than to catch up. He had tried to sleep in a bus station one night, the way he had seen people do in movies, but he had been nervous and self-conscious, and when he saw a policeman, he hurried away and spent most of the night walking around to keep warm. Eventually he had found a department store entrance that was deep enough to protect him from the wind, and he had sat down and leaned against the wall. He had dozed off a little but hadn't really slept much.

But he slept now, soundly, for hours. And then he heard a scream. He spun over on his back, looked around frantically, and tried to think what was happening. The scream came again, faint but strident, and he realized it was on

TV. His body was slow to accept the idea. He was still clinging to the bedspread and breathing hard long after he knew that everything was all right. He looked up, carefully, saw a man on the screen holding a knife, and a woman slinking away from him with her hands over her mouth. He knew she would scream again; he dove across the bed and scrambled onto the floor. Then he stabbed at the "off" button. He didn't wait to watch the light die; he jumped back on the bed and rolled under the covers.

But now the room was black, and he couldn't get his muscles to relax. He held the covers close, and he looked around in the dark, trying to see what was out there. A slice of light was coming under the door, and he could see the dim outline of the furniture at that end of the room. It crossed his mind that someone could be in his room, in the bathroom or lurking in a dark corner.

He thought of the lamp and reached over and turned it on. He could see the room now. He couldn't see the bathroom, but it was stupid to think anyone might be in there. He shouldn't be acting like a baby.

All the same, he was still tense, and he didn't want to shut his eyes yet. He wondered what time it was. He wished now that he had a watch. Then it occurred to him that he could call and find out. He reached over and picked up the phone, still keeping his eyes on the room, as though he expected someone to spring from the closet.

Two one one one. The phone only rang once before he heard, "Front desk."

"Could you tell me what time it is?"

"Let's see. Almost three. Eight minutes till three."

"Thank you."

"Hey, wait. Is this Paul's . . . uh . . . is this David?"

"Yes."

"Are you okay?"

"Yeah."

"Are you scared or anything?"

"No."

"How come you woke up so early?"

"I fell asleep early."

"Are you going back to sleep now?"

David thought about it. "I don't think so."

The guy—Rob—laughed. "Do you want to come down here and have some company for a little while?"

David couldn't think what to say. He liked the man's voice; he didn't want to be alone the rest of the night. But it wasn't a wise thing to do. "No, I guess not."

"You sure? You can come down and get out of that room for a while. You must be getting tired of that place."

"Okay."

"Okay, what? You wanta come down?"

"I guess so." David wondered why he did these things.

"All right. Don't come down by yourself. I'll come up and get you. Get your clothes on and just wait."

A couple minutes later David was sitting at the foot of the bed, all dressed, when a soft knock came on the door. He got up and opened the door. Rob motioned him out and down the hall. He was a young guy, in his twenties, maybe thirty, a little on the heavy side. He was wearing a gold coat, sort of like the one Paul had worn, but no tie.

The elevator opened as soon as Rob pushed the button,

and the two got on. "Okay," Rob said, "let me explain something. Clark is the bellboy who's working tonight. He's an old guy, and he goes to the back of the lobby and 'sits down,' as he calls it. He really sleeps about half the night. He's especially beat tonight because he's been sick the last couple of days. But it might be just as well if he doesn't see you. If no one is in the lobby, we'll go to the front desk, and then I'll open the door to a little office right behind." For no reason that David knew of, Rob began to smile. He had a silly, corners-up kind of grin. "You can sit back there where we can talk to you, but no one who walks through the lobby will see you."

David followed the instructions, but he wondered who the "we" was. As soon as he stepped behind the desk, he found out. A woman, quite an old woman, was sitting at the end of the desk. She had a headset on, with a mouthpiece, like a telephone operator. "This is Elaine," Rob said. "She runs the switchboard, and she does anything she can to drive me crazy all night."

"Hi, David," Elaine said.

David nodded. He was wondering what he had gotten himself into. Rob opened the door to the office, and he set a chair behind the door. "You won't be able to see much," he said, "but you can hear us. And that's just as well. Poor Elaine is so old and ugly, she's not much to look at."

This took David by surprise, but Elaine laughed in a chirping little voice. "Don't lie to the boy. He already saw me. He knows I'm a knockout."

David smiled. These were strange people. He looked around the office and saw a desk with a sign on it that read

"Assistant Manager," and a row of filing cabinets across one wall. He could only see out front through the crack on the hinged side of the door.

He had hardly settled into his chair before Elaine came back to see him. "David, let me look at you and see whether I saw what I think I did." She took his arm and tugged him off the chair. She was a little thing, not much bigger than David, but she crouched and looked him over. "My goodness, you're dirty. These jeans could stand up by themselves. Where have you been sleeping—in the dirt somewhere?"

"It rained one night," David said, surprising himself that he had been so quick to tell her.

"You were out in the rain all night? Where?"

"Down by the farmers' market."

"David! That's a terrible place. Every kind of derelict and dope addict hangs out down there at night."

"Elaine ought to know," Rob said, from out front. "She goes down there trying to pick up guys."

"You can't do this, David. We've got to find a nice place for you to live. Do you hear me?"

David nodded. She was a small, intense woman, like a little bird. She bobbed her head up and down when she talked, but her eyes never lost their fix on his. She was older than David had first thought. She had deep wrinkles along her neck and cheeks, and her upper lip, creased with wrinkles, too, was hairy, the way a teenaged boy's might be. Her hair was dyed an odd sort of red, almost orange, but David could see gray at the roots.

"Are things so bad at home that you can't go back?"

27

"Yes."

"What about your mother? Isn't her heart breaking right now?"

David was getting in too deep. He shook his head and stepped back. Elaine let go.

"I don't mean to scold you. But I'm not letting you spend another night outside. Absolutely not. No matter what, we can do better than that. And I'm bringing you some clean clothes. You can't go around in those things."

Elaine's switchboard began to beep; she went back to it. David sat down, but he didn't know how to react. She could have had his last name in another two minutes, the way she was going. He knew he better not say anything else. He would just sit and listen.

"David, let me tell you something," Rob called through the door. "I promised Paul, if I happened to talk to you, that I wouldn't get nosy. He told me not to ask your last name, and not to ask where you live. So we already understand about that."

David nodded. He could see Rob through the crack. He was not really fat, but the coat he was wearing was too small, and it made his back look meaty. He was pacing back and forth, running an adding machine, and smoking a cigarette in quick puffs.

"So anyway, I just want to ask you two things. What's your last name, and where do you live?"

"Rob!"

"Okay, okay. It's just a joke." He took a puff on his cigarette and set it down. "He knows I'm just kidding. The boy is smart. I could tell that the minute I saw him."

He looked carefully at some papers on the desk for a moment. "He likes my humor, too. I'm a very funny guy. Right now he's cracking up back there. If you looked back there you'd probably find him rolling on the floor, slapping his knees, gasping for air—stuff like that. He's tuned in to me, Elaine. I knew that the minute I saw him."

"No, he's not. He's a nice boy. That's what I saw. He's got big, brown eyes, the size of quarters, and the sweetest face I've ever seen. His hair is a mess right now, but you get him cleaned up and he'd be the cutest boy in Seattle."

"Lay off. You make him sound like a little wimp. I'd say he's more of a man's man—like me. Tough, rugged, good-looking. You know, the strong, silent type."

"Oh, please. He's not anything at all like you. You're a talkative, foul-mouthed, disgusting, chain-smoking maniac. That's what you are."

"Well, true. But at least those are my only faults." Rob picked up his cigarette, took a deep draw on it, and blew the smoke toward Elaine. "David, I need to explain something to you," he said. "We have a nightly ritual around here. Do you know what a ritual is?"

"No."

"Neither does he," Elaine said. "He just tries to use big words to impress people."

"I know exactly what a ritual is. I'm a college-educated man. I went to college almost two years before I flunked out."

"Tell the truth. You quit."

"Same thing."

"No, it isn't. You could have done anything you

29

wanted, but you quit." Then, in a slightly louder voice, "David, he's very smart, but he never finishes anything."

"One other thing you need to know, David," Rob said. "Elaine is madly in love with me. It's really disgusting to see how she longs for a young man like me. Of course, I understand it, because I am exceptionally good-looking, but I still think it's a sad thing when an extremely old person falls for an extremely young person—and won't give up."

"Well, now, most of that's true," Elaine said. "I am madly in love with the boy, and he is very young, and he is good-looking." David didn't really think that was true. "But I'm not so old as you might think. I'm actually thirty-five, and not a day over."

"Yeah, yeah. Right. David, listen, as you can see, the woman lies. And anyway, she changed the subject and I still haven't told you about our ritual."

But someone had come into the lobby now. Rob and Elaine greeted the man, whom David couldn't see. He didn't come to the desk. He said, "Whatever you do, don't give me a wake-up call," and he apparently walked to the elevators.

Rob waited until the man was gone before he said, "Okay, here's the deal. Every night between three and four or so—once the place really quiets down—"

"Sometimes earlier, when you're hungry."

"All right. All right. Don't get so technical. But anyway, David, I go down to the kitchen and make a fresh pot of coffee. And while it's brewing, I go across the street to the place where all the—"

"Rob, don't you say that. David doesn't have to hear that kind of talk."

"Okay, I won't say who hangs out at the place across the street. But it's a greasy little diner that does happen to make very nice pie. Now . . . I'm going to give you an important list, and I want you to consider it carefully."

David waited. He didn't know what Rob was talking about.

"Cherry. Lemon. Blueberry. Apple. Coconut. Pecan. And this time of year, pumpkin. Consider that list for exactly two minutes and then give me your first three choices in order of preference. In about ten minutes you will be feasting on your favorite pie—or at least your second or third choice."

"Ask him who pays for it almost every night. That's part of the ritual, too. He won't ever let me pay."

"David, this woman is senile. She pays every single night. She never remembers that. But tonight, just to prove that I'm right, I'll let her pay again. Now, everyone be quiet. David is thinking. Elaine, get your money out."

David was smiling. These were the strangest people he had ever known. But he liked listening to them.

"Okay, David," Rob said.

"That wasn't two minutes," Elaine said.

"Be quiet. He's a fast thinker. First choice?"

"I already ate quite a bit last night, and—"

"I accept no such answer, and neither does Elaine, and she's paying."

"That's right."

"First choice?"

"Lemon."

"Second?"

"Cherry."

"Okay. That's enough. They always have at least one of those."

"They have boysenberry, too," Elaine said. "Sometimes they do."

"Hush, woman. Don't confuse the boy. Their boysenberry pie tastes like . . . cow pies."

"Watch your tongue, young man."

"Hey, you should have heard what I was going to say."

"I know what you were going to say. David, he has a filthy mouth. I'm a delicate little lady, a senior citizen, and this boy talks dirty in front of me all the time."

"Yeah, right. She taught me everything I know, David." And away he went, telling Elaine to have the money ready when he came back from making the coffee.

Elaine laughed and then she said, "David, come out here for just a minute. I want to tell you something."

David got up and walked to the door. He preferred staying back where he had been.

"Just a minute. I've got to make a wake-up call. Some of these poor people have to get up so early—to catch flights and all."

David had a moment to look around the lobby. It was nice, not big and open like hotels he had seen in movies, but fancy and old-fashioned, with marble and dark wood paneling on the walls, and classy-looking old paintings and hanging plants. Directly across the lobby was a desk with a "Bell Captain" sign on it, and behind that a closed door.

Nearby, to the left, was a hallway with a sign overhead that said "Dining Room."

"Okay," Elaine said, "you watch when Rob comes back. He won't stop here. He'll go buy the pie. He does that every night. He hardly ever gives me a chance to pay."

Somehow that didn't really surprise David.

"Rob's the best there is. And he's telling the truth when he says I'm in love with him. Two years ago I thought I was dying. He came to work here and I felt better almost the first night. I'm glad every night to come down here now. He keeps me laughing, and he won't let me feel sorry for myself a single minute. He's rough as a cob, and he does have a foul mouth, but I love that boy."

David nodded, but he hardly knew what to think of all this.

"Your friend Paul is a good man, too. I guess he's had his problems, from what people say, but I've never known him to be anything but a gentleman. He trades jokes with Rob, but he treats me so respectful it almost embarrasses me. I could love that man, too. He's better looking than Rob and closer to my age. Ain't I awful?"

David laughed. He didn't say anything, but he already knew he didn't think she was awful. He returned to the back room and sat down, while Elaine laughed.

And then Rob came striding through the lobby, saying, "Let's see, David wanted banana cream or else boysenberry."

David smiled, by himself, in the little office. And Rob didn't stop for any money. Elaine was right about that.

At about five-thirty, David had to go back upstairs. Rob said that quite a few people started to stir around about that time, and it would be just as well if no one saw him. When David got to the room, he turned on the television set and watched the end of a really stupid movie. He seemed to notice the loneliness of the room more now. At some point he got out his pocketknife, opened and shut the blades a few times, and then just held it as he watched TV.

Right after seven o'clock Rob brought him up some breakfast, and about an hour later Paul called. "Are you okay?" he asked.

"Yeah."

"You're not planning to take off, are you?"

"Not yet." He had told himself he really wouldn't stay the whole weekend, that he would slip out sometime.

Now he wondered how Paul knew that—or at least suspected it.

"Okay. I'll be in this afternoon. I'll talk to you then. Alberto will bring you lunch."

"Okay." David put down the phone. He looked at his clothes piled on the chair by the door. He knew he should go now. Paul would just keep pressuring him. But he decided to stay where he was warm for a while yet. He soon fell asleep again. In fact, he slept most of the day. That afternoon Paul came by. He sat in the chair where he had sat the day before. He was wearing the same gray jacket, but he had on a white shirt, a turtleneck. His skin looked dark against the bright white of the shirt, and his hair looked rather long, hanging over the collar a little. David had some sense that Paul had been dressing the same way for a long time, that he was clinging to something.

"Were you asleep?" Paul asked.

"Sort of, I guess."

"I talked to Rob this morning. He said you went down there for a while last night."

David nodded.

"I guess Elaine's ready to adopt you. Rob says she really likes you."

David was embarrassed. He shrugged. It was not just Elaine's words, it was the gentle stroke of Paul's voice, too. He knew that for some reason Paul liked him.

"I wish she could take you. Poor old gal—she's been alone forty, fifty years, something like that."

"Why?"

35

"I'm not sure. She was married once, but her husband died. Probably in the war or something. I never got the whole story. I don't think she's ever had much. She's had to get by the best she could."

"Does she have any kids?"

"I don't think so. Not that I know of. She lives in a little apartment over north of the canal somewhere. Not much of a life." And then Paul laughed. "I should talk. I live in a run-down old hotel around the corner from here. It's a dump."

"Why do you live there then?" David didn't have the feeling that Paul was poor.

Paul smiled, looking past David. "Well, that's kind of a long story." He leaned back, put his hands behind his head.

"I've made some pretty good money in my day, and I've lived in some nice places. When I was working the St. Francis, I made some really good bucks. Bellboys do okay if they're in the right kind of house. The first year I worked there I bought me a brand-new Buick. Paid cash. And then every year after that, five years in a row, I bought me another new one. Just brought in the old one and paid cash for the difference." Paul smiled much broader than he usually did, his head still back. David could see that he was missing a tooth on the side.

"I made real good money. I also spent good money. And I got into some bad habits back in those days." His eyes met David's for just a second. "I got to be a real drunk, David. I used to work the dogleg shift—eleven in the morning till seven at night. That gave me all night to party. I made money every day, and I spent it every night. If there's anything really stupid a man can do, I probably did it in those days. I eventually got fired at the St. Francis, and I got run out of half the hotels in San Francisco. Over the years, I worked Vegas and Reno and Tahoe. Sooner or later I got fired from all of 'em. And I also ruined my liver. If I drink now, my doctor says it'll kill me. In fact, I almost did die. I was in a hospital almost a month, just before I came up here."

"But you don't drink at all now?"

"Nope. I'm forty-three years old and all used up. There's not a whole lot I can do. The only thing I ever did all those years was drink and party and hang around bars. Now I gotta drink soda pop. So I came up here—mostly to get away from all my drinking buddies. And I figure I better save my money. I haven't saved a dime in my life until this year. I've got to start putting aside something. So that's why I live where I do. It doesn't cost much, and I don't figure I need that much."

"You're not very happy, are you?"

Paul smiled and then gradually let the smile fade. But he didn't answer for some time. "Well, I'll tell you, David. If I drink I'm going to die. But if I don't drink, I don't know what to live for. That sounds stupid to a kid like you. But I don't have anybody. I go see my mom at a rest home—once a week—and I have a couple of lady friends, but no one I care anything about. I guess I feel like I quit living last year."

"You shouldn't feel that way."

Paul looked at David curiously. "Well, you're a fine one

to talk. You hightailed it from somewhere to nowhere. You don't even know where you're going."

"I'm going to California."

"Oh, you are? And why California?" But David didn't answer. He already wished he could take it back. He didn't want anyone to know his plan.

"You figure it's warmer down there? If you get stuck outside at night, you won't get cold?"

David shrugged. The truth was, that was exactly what he had thought.

"What part of California?"

"I don't know."

"How about San Francisco—my old town?"

"Maybe."

"That shows what you know, David. That place is just as cold as Seattle is now, year-round. How are you going to get to California anyway?"

"I'll find a way."

Paul laughed, making almost no noise. "David, it won't work."

David shrugged again. He looked over at the TV. He wanted Paul to leave.

"Look, I'm sorry to preach at you so much. I hated it when people did that to me when I was a kid. But I'm asking you questions you have to figure out some answers to. I'll just leave it at that."

After Paul left, David watched television for a while, and then he fell asleep again. And he knew why. He wanted to go down to the front desk. He wanted to be with Rob and Elaine.

It was two-thirty when he finally called Rob, but he had been awake for an hour. Rob came up for him again. And when the two got to the desk, the first thing Elaine did was hand David a paper bag, full of clothes. "Go back in the office and change," she said. "There's two pair of jeans and four shirts. Pick out what you like. I bought them at Goodwill. But they're just like new. I hope they fit all right."

When David showed up at the door, wearing a striped T-shirt and a pair of the jeans, she was thrilled. "Well, the jeans are a little big, I guess, but better that than too small. How old are you anyway, David? I didn't know what to tell the lady at the store."

"Eleven," David said, surprised that he had told the truth.

"Well, that's about what I thought. But you could be ten, just as easy. You'll take off like a shot one of these days, and then we'll be glad we bought these just a little big." She was turning him around, looking him over, front and back, and she tugged the jeans up higher. "Can't you roll those up? Do the boys do that now?"

"I guess so," David said, but he wasn't sure. He didn't pay much attention to what other boys did with their clothes.

"No way," Rob said. "He doesn't want to roll the things up. Can't you whack off about four inches and then sew 'em up or something?"

"Well, sure. Let's see if the other pair is just the same. You can wear these rolled up for one day. I can fix one pair tomorrow, and the other one the next day." She got the other pair and held them up alongside the ones he had on. Then she had to have him try on each of the shirts.

When David was finally sitting behind the door, quiet again, he felt very strange, tingly up and down his back. He hadn't been fussed over like that in a long time. But he was thinking of his mother now, and he knew he couldn't do that.

Rob kept telling Elaine what a crazy old lady she was. "It's bad enough you're in love with a young guy like me; now you've gone and fallen in love with an eleven-year-old boy. You know how I can tell? You wore your new dress tonight—trying to look good for the kid."

"That's right. I did. What's wrong with that?" David had noticed the dress, printed with little flowers, and with a white collar. And her hair had been fixed up nicer than the night before. David had smelled something sweet in her hair when she leaned close to him. Maybe she had gone to one of those places to have it done.

"Hey, I know he's handsome, but, lady, you don't have a chance. He's got girls hanging all over him. He's the most popular kid at his school. I can see that just by looking at him."

"It's school that worries me, David," Elaine said, ignoring Rob. "How many days have you missed now?"

David had to count up, had to think what day it was. It was Saturday night, or actually, Sunday morning. He had left Tuesday evening—Wednesday, Thursday, Friday. "Three," he finally said.

"Oh, David. This just isn't good. It makes me cry when I think of it. A boy your age just can't afford to miss school—not any days at all."

40

David resolved again that he had to be more careful with Elaine. She was moving in on him. He couldn't let her make his decisions.

"Hey, David, tonight I'm going to introduce you to another ritual. Well, no. This is not a ritual. This I would call a tradition. I do it only once in a while—on nights when I just can't stand this place any longer. And tonight is such a night."

"Rob," Elaine said, "I know exactly what you're talking about. But you're not going to start messing around with my switchboard again. I won't let you."

"David, I'm going to have to hurt this old lady. Don't look. Things might get pretty ugly." In a moment there was a scuffle, Elaine laughing and apparently slapping at Rob. All the while, Rob was saying, "Take that, you old bird. Pow. Take that. Pow."

And then in a few more seconds, he said, "Okay, David, come on out. I killed her."

David went out and found Rob at the switchboard, with the earphones, Elaine standing behind him. "He's going to ruin my machine sometime," she said, but she was smiling, her little yellow teeth all showing.

"Be quiet," Rob said. "Okay, now here's what we do. I call a night auditor at a downtown hotel. That's the person at the desk at night—like me. Then, quickly, while the phone is ringing, I call another one. One answers and starts saying, 'Hello, hello,' and then the other answers and I plug the two of 'em in together." Rob was looking down a list of numbers, and then he dialed. "Okay, David, step up here, quick." Rob lifted the earphones from his head and slid them over David's ears. "Okay, listen now."

David pulled the earphones on straight, so the little earpieces were sitting right. He heard a man say, "Shorefront Hotel," and then, "Hello. Hello?" Just then a woman said, "Seattle Hilton."

"Hello?"

"Yes, this is the Hilton. May I help you?"

"Uh . . . no. You called me."

"What? Who is this?"

"This is the Shorefront. What can I do for you?"

"You called me."

"No, I'm sorry. I didn't call anyone. The phone rang and I picked it up, and you were on the line."

"No, not at all. My phone rang and I picked it up."

A silence followed. David was smiling, looking up at Rob, who was grinning hugely. There was something very boyish about him. His hair always fell forward, almost in his eyes, and he smiled almost all the time. "Is it working?" he asked. David nodded. Rob pulled one earpiece away from David's ear and bent close, so he could listen.

"Well, I can't imagine why my phone would ring. Are you sure you weren't calling someone and dialed the wrong number?"

"No. I was just standing here working on the audit, and the phone rang."

"Same here. I do the audit at the Shorefront."

"That's weird. I mean, really weird. Could it be a short in the wiring, or . . ."

"No. I don't . . . think so."

Suddenly Rob whispered, "Okay, watch this." He pulled the earphones off David's head and put them on his

42

own, but he held out one earpiece and motioned for David to hold it and listen. Then he pressed a button and said, "Hello, Sheraton Hotel. May I help you?"

Both people were silent for a moment, and then the woman said, "What in the world is going on?"

"Going on?" Rob said. "I'm sure I don't know. Did you call me to ask what is going on? This is a hotel, not an information bureau. I'm afraid I do not keep a calendar of current events here at the desk."

"No, no," they were saying at the same time. And then the man said, "We were both standing here and our phones rang. We were trying to figure out what was going on, and then you came on."

"Listen, I'm very busy," Rob said. "I don't need prank calls in the middle of the night. Please get off my line." He pulled both cords from the board and burst out laughing.

"He's a lunatic," Elaine said.

Rob had his head down on the panel. He was roaring, his shoulders bouncing. "That was great," he said. "That was perfect. 'Maybe it's a short in the wiring.' What an idiot." His big voice boomed through the lobby.

David was laughing, too, but mostly because of Rob. And then without warning, Rob stopped laughing and slid off the chair. "All right, it's time for some pie," he said. "Let's see, David, you're a peach man, as I recall. Sorry, we're all out of that. Have you tried our chocolate? We're out of that, too. Elaine, don't you think it's about time you let me pay?" And away he went to the kitchen.

5

~~~~~~~~

Rob paid for the pie again. After he ate he said he was going to call some more hotels, but Elaine said she wouldn't let him. About then a man in a bellman's uniform came walking out of the back lobby. David was standing at the front desk, eating his pie and drinking a big glass of milk. He wasn't sure what he should do, but it was too late to make a dash. He knew it had to be Clark.

"Hello, Clark," Rob said, without the slightest note of concern. "This is our friend, David. He's a lemon meringue man. Want some pie?"

"No, thanks."

Clark showed no signs of disapproval. He was an older man, kind of small and neat, except for big gray eyebrows that hung down over his eyes. He looked tired, the dark skin under his eyes drooping into little wrinkled pouches.

"Clark's the only millionaire who works here, David," Rob said. "He's never spent a dime in his life. He takes every penny home and hides it in his mattress. He can't even sleep on the thing, it's so full of money. That's why he works the night shift."

Clark shook his head, smiled ever so little, and then walked across the lobby to the bellmen's desk. He opened the door behind it and went inside.

"I'll talk to him," Elaine whispered. "He won't say anything if I talk to him."

But David wasn't looking at Elaine. A woman—a girl—was coming toward the desk. David didn't know where she had come from.

"Melissa, what are you still doing here?" Rob said.

She was looking at David. "Who's this?"

"David. He's a friend of ours."

David looked down at the desk. He thought the girl was very pretty.

"David, this is Melissa. She works in the bar, serving Seattle's fine gentlemen the best in alcoholic beverages."

"David, who are you?" Her voice was quiet, almost tender. She had long hair—light brown—and pretty, soft-looking skin.

"David is Paul's friend, and that's all we better say. If anyone asks, say that you don't remember seeing any eleven-year-old kids eating lemon meringue pie at the front desk in the middle of the night."

"Paul's friend?"

Elaine had gotten up from her chair and had come over next to David, who had now stepped back a little from the desk. Elaine patted Melissa's hand. "I'll tell you about it another time. What are you still doing here anyway?"

"I don't know. I was just sitting down there with

45

Sharon. Talking. Drinking coffee. Which is stupid, since I need to go home and get some sleep."

David looked again. Melissa didn't seem old enough to work in a bar. She looked like a teenager. She was wearing a blue shirt, like a boy's, with a button-down collar, and a darker blue jacket over that. Her eyes were blue, too, and dark, like her jacket.

"I'll tell you what you need to do, little girl," Elaine said. "You need to get married."

"Yeah, well, I already tried that once."

"That's what I used to say, too. I didn't want to jump right back into another marriage, I said, and now it's forty-six years later, and I'm all alone. Don't do that to yourself."

"I don't exactly meet the sort of guys I want to settle down with, not around here."

"Wait just a minute," Rob said. "How many times have I asked you to marry me?"

"I don't know. At least a hundred." She smiled a little brighter, her eyes opening wide for the first time.

"I'd say more like five hundred. At least twice a night, five nights a week, since you started working here."

She leaned against the desk and reached out and took hold of Rob's lapel. "Okay. What if I said yes one of these times? You'd move out of town the next morning."

"Try me."

But Elaine was laughing. "You've got him pegged, Melissa. He goes with a girl until she starts to like him. Then he heads for cover."

"Hey, all of them like me. I'm just not selfish enough to give myself to one woman."

But Melissa was looking at David again. "You're sure cute," she said. "Do you care if I tell you that?"

David knew he was blushing. He wished she wouldn't look at him.

"What happened to that guy you were going with?" Elaine asked.

"Who? Gary?"

"The policeman."

"Yeah, Gary. He decided to go back to his wife."

"The guy's out of his mind," Rob said.

"He asked me to marry him—about as many times as you have. But there was no chance."

"Why, honey?" Elaine asked. "Oh, just a minute." She walked over to the switchboard and answered a call.

Melissa waited, smiling a little, looking down. "I don't need another guy like my first husband," she said as Elaine was coming back.

"Why? What was he like?"

Melissa laughed, softly. "Well, he was good-looking—like Gary. And he was big and strong, like Gary. He was also stupid, like Gary."

"Where did you meet him anyway?"

"My ex-husband? Or Gary?"

"Your ex-husband."

"I met him in my hometown in Minnesota. But he wasn't from there." For some reason, she kept looking at David, which was unnerving. David could only look at her in little peeks. "He came there one summer working on a construction crew. I was seventeen years old. This friend of mine used to go walk with me past the building he was working on, just to have a look at some of these young guys who were on the crew. That was big stuff to us—having somebody to look at besides the pimply faced boys at the high school."

"Have you noticed how clear my complexion is?" Rob said. Melissa glanced at him and shook her head, smiling. "So anyway, one day a couple of the guys talked to us a little, and Jack—the guy I later married—asked me to go out. He was some talker. We went out all that summer—even though my parents were really against it—and he kept telling me all the great stuff he was going to do. For one thing, he told me he was moving out here to Seattle. It all sounded great compared to staying around there and marrying some local kid in town. But it almost killed my parents when I took off with him. I still had a year of high school left. I just went and then called them when I got out here. I've never been back home, either. I'm not sure I would even be welcome."

David expected Rob to make another joke, but he didn't. Elaine said, "You'd be welcome, honey. People don't hold a mistake against you forever."

"What happened to this Jack guy?" Rob asked.

"Who knows? We got out here and the job he thought he had fell through. Everything was a mess. He had sunk every penny he had into a big, fancy car. We both got jobs after a while, but we hadn't been married more than a couple of months before he was looking around at other girls. And then one day he just left. I came home from work and his clothes were all gone. He cleared out the checkbook, didn't leave me a penny. I've never seen him since. The only good thing was I never had a baby. And that was just luck." She looked at David. "I shouldn't talk like that around you," she said. "How old are you? Are you really eleven?"

"Yeah."

"What are you doing up so late?"

David hesitated, and Rob said, "Eating pie, of course. Can't you see? Hey, David, your milk's getting warm. You better finish it." Actually, David hadn't once thought of his food since Melissa had appeared.

"I gotta go," Melissa said. "Good-night, David. I guess no one's going to tell me who you are. Maybe I'll see you again sometime." She walked away.

Rob watched her, and then he sighed. "I think the finest single experience in life is watching that girl walk through this lobby wearing jeans."

"You be respectful, Rob. That's the sweetest girl in this world," Elaine said.

"Oh, believe me, I respect everything about her. Her face, her hair, her voice, her body, her—"

"Rob, I'm serious. She's pretty, but she's a lovely girl, too, and she hasn't had a decent break in her whole life."

David ate the rest of his pie, drank his milk. And then he got up the nerve to say, "Do you really want to marry Melissa, Rob?"

David had never before spoken to one of them without being spoken to. His question seemed to take both Rob and Elaine by surprise. It was Elaine who answered. "Melissa knows what she's talking about. Rob's too scared to get married."

Rob smiled a little, glanced over at David, but he didn't

say anything. He was clicking a pencil against the marble desk top, seeming hardly aware of the little rhythm he was making.

"He likes girls. There's hardly anything else he does like. But he doesn't want to stick with one all the time."

"Why should I?" Rob said, and he sounded sort of serious.

"Because that's the best thing there is in life—having a family. Having someone to come home to. Having a little boy to teach to play baseball, or a little girl to buy a pretty dress for. That's the only thing that matters even a little bit in this world. I had just enough of it to know, and then I lost it. So listen to what I keep telling you." She looked over at David and said, "I tell him every night, but he doesn't listen to me." She tried to smile, but David saw the wetness that had slipped into the wrinkles at the corners of her eyes. He was surprised.

"Well, I'll tell you," Rob said. He was looking across the lobby, leaning forward with his elbows on the desk. "I grew up a lot like Melissa. Idaho. Little town. Meat and potatoes for supper. But my old man hated my mother for twenty-eight years, and she hated him—until they finally got a divorce. They thought they were staying together for me and my brothers. What a joke. I guess I don't have such a pretty idea about marriage as you do."

Elaine went back to her chair and sat down. She picked up her headset but didn't put it on. No one said anything, until she spoke softly. "It doesn't have to be like that," she said.

David wondered. He tried to picture a dad who came

50

home from work and said, "Let's go play some baseball." He saw the fathers like that on TV all the time; he wondered whether that wasn't like a lot of things—only on TV or in the movies.

At five-thirty David went upstairs. But he felt the loneliness again. He turned on the television set and tried to lose himself in a movie, but he couldn't even think what was happening. There was a pretty girl in the film, but not half as pretty as Melissa. He didn't think he had ever seen a girl quite as pretty as Melissa.

He thought of Rob, too. And Elaine. He had thought they just had fun all the time. He felt strange now, knowing something more about them. David had never really gotten to know any adults, not to understand anything about their feelings. Why would they talk to him about such things? Paul had done the same thing.

And then the worst thought struck him. He tried to force it away, but he knew it was true. He didn't want to leave the hotel. Not now.

6

David fell asleep watching television. When he heard someone at the door, he assumed it was Alberto bringing lunch, but he was stunned when a maid came walking into the room, and she was just as surprised to be looking at him. "Oh, excuse me, I thought this room was vacant," she said.

David sat up, suddenly, but then froze. He felt the panic swelling in him, but he couldn't think what to do. The maid was looking at him, curiously, apparently sensing that something wasn't right. She was a thin woman, black but very light, with freckles around her eyes. "You here alone?" she asked, and she glanced around.

David said nothing. He thought of running, but he had his shoes off, and his coat was in the closet. The maid was still looking around, obviously aware that no luggage was about, no parents. "What's going on here?" she asked.

David couldn't think of anything to say. He didn't want to get Paul into trouble. But his silence seemed to prove to her that something was wrong. She walked to the little table by David's bed and picked up the phone. After a moment she said, "Yeah, this is Mary. I'm up in seven-oh-four. Have you got anyone registered in here?"

By now David was thinking about police coming. He got out of bed slowly, got his shoes, and then sat in the chair and began to put them on. He hoped that when he got to the lobby he could make a run.

"You just sit right there," the maid said. And then, into the phone, "Out of order? Well, then, what's a young boy doing up here all by himself? Do you know anything about that?" She paused, listened, and then said, "I don't know. He won't say a thing."

In a moment she said, "That's fine," and put down the phone. She had never taken her eyes off David. Now she said, "Well, boy, I don't know what's going on, but I do know you shouldn't be up here. Someone's coming up."

David was thinking ahead. What would he say to the police? He would keep his mouth shut, but the Poulters would have reported him missing—no doubt about that—and it wouldn't take much to figure out who he was.

In a few minutes a guy showed up—a balding man in a bellman's uniform who talked louder than he needed to. He was wearing a name tag that read, "Ralph," and under that, "Captain." He nodded to Mary. "So what's the deal?" he said.

"I don't know. I was out of towels, and I come in here looking for some, thinking this was a vacant room, and

53

then I see this boy, sleeping with the TV on. He won't say a word, but he don't have a blessed thing with him—'cept that sack. Betty said the room was marked down 'out of order.' "

Ralph picked up the paper sack and looked in. "Shirts," he said. "That's all." And then he looked down at David again and spoke rather gruffly. "So what's going on, kid? What's your name?"

"I'll leave now," David said. "I didn't hurt anything." He stood up. He could feel himself shaking, but he didn't want them to see that.

"How long you been in here?"

David didn't answer.

"Did you sneak in or something?" He had a strange way of talking, as though his upper lip were deadened.

No matter what, David wasn't getting Paul into trouble. "If I can have my coat, I'll just leave." He took a step toward the closet.

Ralph was closer. He got the coat and said, "Let's go downstairs. I'll let someone else figure this one out." Then he swore and turned to Mary. "This is a new one on me." He smiled a little, his upper lip still not moving. David had sensed all along that the gruffness was something of an act, but he still didn't trust this guy.

David picked up his shirts and went with Ralph. He took David by the arm and walked him to the elevator. He didn't let go as they waited, not even in the elevator.

"Okay, Betty," Ralph said, as he walked David across the lobby, "here's your criminal. I think we've got us a stowaway. He must've snuck in the room somehow."

Betty was at the front desk. She was a big woman, tall and quite heavy. She was wearing a purple dress that hung straight down. She leaned over on the desk, with her elbows under her, smiled slowly, winked, and said, "You don't look like much of a criminal." David felt safer with her, but he was still scared.

"He won't say who he is," Ralph said. He still had hold of David's arm, up high, by the shoulder.

"Won't you tell me your name?" Betty asked.

"I just slept in that room last night," David said. "I'm sorry. I'll go now. Can I have my coat?"

"Where do you live?"

David shrugged. He didn't know what else to do.

"Are you a runaway?"

David looked at the front of the desk, not at Betty. If only he could grab his coat and run. He didn't want to go through all this again.

"We better call the cops," Ralph said.

David glanced at Betty. He could see that she was considering, not so certain as Ralph as to what they should do. Her face was fleshy and sort of pretty, but with more makeup than David liked. "Are you telling me you just walked into this hotel, went upstairs, and went to bed?"

David nodded.

"How did you get into the room?"

"The door was open."

Betty looked a little doubtful, but she didn't say so. A man had approached the desk, wanting to check out. "Come back here," Betty said to David, motioning him to come behind the desk. And then she said to Ralph, "Let's let Mr. Raymond talk to him. He called and said he'd be coming in before long."

"It don't matter to me," Ralph said. He let go of David, reached into his inside coat pocket, got out a pack of cigarettes. "I'll set his coat over in the bellmen's room." He walked away.

David walked behind the desk and stood behind Betty while she took care of the man who was checking out. "So what do you think of this?" she said to the man. "This little boy walked in here last night and slept in one of our rooms. What do you suppose we ought to do with him?"

"Throw him in jail," the man said, laughing as though he had just said something really clever.

Betty turned around and took another look at David. "I don't know. I think I'd rather keep him. Have you ever seen prettier eyes than that? He's got eyelashes any girl would like to have."

David was bothered by the teasing, but he had a feeling Betty was on his side.

When the man left, she turned around and said, "Mr. Raymond is our assistant manager. He usually comes in late on Sundays. But he should get here before too long. I don't know what to do but let him decide what to do with you." She shook her head slowly, smiling down at him. "What I'd like to do is give you a great big hug. You look scared enough to die right on the spot. Can't you tell me who you are, honey?"

David didn't say anything. He was wondering what to expect from this Raymond guy.

"Don't be scared. No one's going to do anything to you. Why don't you just tell me your name?"

David wasn't going to do that again. He looked away. She smiled more brightly. "No name, huh?"

David had just spotted Alberto coming to the desk. He shook his head, trying to let Alberto know that he shouldn't say anything.

"Oh, wow," Alberto said. "Did you find this kid in the hotel somewhere?"

"Yes. In a room," Betty said. "Do you know something about him?"

"Maybe. What did he tell you?"

"Not much. He said he came in and found a door open and slept in the hotel last night. What do you know about it?"

David shook his head at Alberto again. "Well, nothing. I don't know nothing myself." He stopped and thought. "What are you going to do with him?"

"I don't know. I'm going to see what Mr. Raymond says. He'll probably have to call the police. I'm pretty sure he's a runaway. But tell me what you know."

Alberto was thinking again. "Well, I'll just say this, and I won't say nothing else. Call Paul. Ask him what he thinks you ought to do."

"What does Paul have to do with it?"

"Maybe nothing. Maybe something. You ask him."

Betty shrugged, her big shoulders rising slowly, and then she picked up the phone. She seemed to know the number.

"Paul," she said, "sorry to call you so early. I know you like your beauty sleep." She laughed, deeply. "Let me ask you something. Do you know anything about a little boy sleeping up in room seven-oh-four?"

Betty listened a moment and then explained how the maid had found him. After that she listened for a long time. Once she said, "Paul, you took a big chance," but mostly she heard him out. David felt sick. He knew what Paul had to be thinking—that David had told on him.

"I don't know, Paul. Ralph knows all about this. You know he's going to hit the ceiling. All I can do is tell him what you said. I don't know whether he'll go for it. You better come over and talk to him yourself."

She listened again, agreed to whatever he said, and then she put the phone down. She looked at David. "Well," she said, exhaling, "the old stuff is going to hit the fan now." She reached down and hit the button that rang an electronic bell. In a moment David saw Ralph come out of the bellmen's room, shut the door, and walk across the lobby.

"Okay, Ralph," Betty said, as he approached, "listen to me for a minute. Don't start yelling until I'm all finished."

"What are you talking about?"

"I just talked to Paul. The other night, when he was working the night shift, he found this boy—his name is David—up in a hallway sleeping by the Coke machine. He let him into that room."

Ralph said a vile word, doubled a fist, and shook it. "Okay, that's it. Paul's finally given me a good reason. He's out of here."

"Quiet down." Betty motioned with her head toward some people who had just gotten off the elevator. "You don't have to tell the whole world. Now, just listen to me for a second, all right?

"He says you can do what you want about that, but he doesn't want us to turn the boy over to anybody. Paul will be over as soon as he can. In the meantime, he said to let David sit in the bellmen's room."

Ralph swore again, said the same word. "What does the man think we're running here? This ain't no home for runaway kids."

Betty shushed him as a couple came toward the desk. Ralph stepped to the side and suddenly realized that the people had baggage. He was quick to take it from them, and he assured them that he could have a taxi for them in "no time at all." He carried the suitcases to the front doors and then came back and used a phone at the bellmen's desk. Betty chatted with the people as she checked them out, but she didn't mention David this time.

Once the couple was gone, Ralph came back to the desk. He was about to say something when Betty spoke first. "Ralph, look at this boy. Does he look like a troublemaker to you? Paul took one look at him and felt sorry for him, the same as anyone would. He's been trying to figure something out, someplace to send him. He's going to talk to a social worker on Monday and see what can be done."

"Let me tell you something, Betty. I spent seventeen years of my life working carnivals. I—"

"I know that, Ralph. That's the only thing you ever talk about."

"Just listen to me for a second, will you?" David could see that Betty's words had irritated him. "The kid who sneaks around your back and steals your prizes—or slips

59

a hand in your cash drawer—he's always the kid with a baby face and big old teddy-bear eyes. And if you grab him, right in the act, he's got a sob story about coming from a bad home life. That's the biggest con around."

"Look, Ralph, you believe whatever you want. But just take David over to the bellmen's room and let him sit there. Paul's coming over. After you talk to Paul, do what you want. All he's asking is that you wait until he gets here."

"Betty, I'll do what I gotta do. Paul's not talking me into anything. The guy thinks he can get around me no matter what he does. He never has believed that I'm his boss."

"Whatever, Ralph. Don't get me into all that. But Paul is trying to find a place for this boy. I don't see anything wrong with that."

"Are you telling me you don't see anything wrong with opening up a door and letting someone sleep in the hotel? Especially a runaway kid? There's laws against stuff like that."

"I know that, Ralph. Paul shouldn't have done it. I'm just not sure I would have done any different."

Ralph still had his fist doubled, stuck against his hip. "Well, that may be how you look at it. But I don't. And Paul made up his own rules, the way he always does. This time I think I'm going to fire him. Come on, kid. You can sit over here for a few minutes. But that ain't changing nothing. Paul's pushed me once too often."

David glanced at Betty as he left the desk. She winked at him. Ralph had walked on ahead. "He yells a lot, but he won't do anything," she said. "He never does."

7

David sat on a rather high stool in the bellmen's room. It was the closest thing to a chair that was in there. The room was small and dark, and too warm. David didn't like the powerful smell of cigarette smoke, didn't like waiting, but mostly he didn't like Ralph staying so close. He sat at the bellmen's desk, just outside the door, apparently feeling that he had to keep a watch on David.

"What kind of story did you lay on Paul? You must have done some con job on him."

David didn't answer.

"I'll tell you something, kid. Paul thinks he's better than everybody around here. He's worked the St. Francis—as he never stops telling everybody. He's worked Vegas and Tahoe. He thinks that makes him some kind of big shot. The truth is, the guy's nothing but a broken-down drunk. I'm sure he put on a big show for you—played the role like he's trying to save your life—but he ain't nobody you can trust. You're a lot better off with the cops."

David didn't want to listen to this. He hoped that if he said nothing, Ralph would shut up, maybe even walk away.

"You don't talk much, do you?"

"No."

"I guess you're scared, huh?"

"No." David was so scared his stomach was sick, but he wasn't about to say that to Ralph.

"Yeah, well, I don't believe that." He pulled his pack of cigarettes from his pocket. "I ran away from home once. I was about your age. I lasted about two hours, and then I got hungry and went back." He laughed, harder than usual, and his top lip slipped up a little. David saw his front teeth, badly decayed, with jagged gaps between them. He suddenly realized why Ralph laughed the way he did. "How long you been on the run?"

David didn't answer. He didn't see why he should.

"Hey, look, kid, you don't have to be afraid of me. I ain't gonna say anything to anybody. Maybe you think I'm some kind of jerk because I want to turn you over to the cops, but I just happen to think that's the best thing for you. That don't mean I got it in for you. You understand what I'm saying to you?"

Ralph waited, lit the cigarette, took a long drag on it, and then blew the smoke out. He tossed the match on the floor. David thought he was older than Paul. The skin around his eyes and under his jaw looked leathery, even had a dirty look to it. "Let me tell you something you might as well learn right now. Think about it this way. There's something you want from me, isn't there? Tell me what that is."

David hesitated, but finally he said, "I don't want anything from you."

"Yes, but you do. You want me not to call the cops. Right?"

"Yes."

"Okay. Now, if you want to get something from me, you oughta be thinking what you can do to get it from me. You gotta figure me out. You gotta play me along and see what works. The trouble is, you're a little kid, so you don't think it through that good. And I don't mean no insult by that." He glanced back and smiled, his lip stiff again.

David looked away.

"But see, you're playing it wrong. The first thing you oughta do is maybe put a story on me—tell me what a bad deal you've got at home. Your old lady is raising you alone and ain't fed you in a week. She's drunk, or she's got some disease—or something. See what I'm saying? It's worth a shot. What you'd find out, of course, is that I'm an old con man—a carney—and I ain't going for it. But you give it a shot. Do you see what I'm telling you?" When David didn't answer, he asked again.

"Yes," David finally said.

Ralph took another draw on his cigarette and then set it down on an ashtray. "Okay, so that don't work. So you figure maybe you can talk real nice. Maybe you can get talking to me and I start liking you, and then maybe I'll say, 'Ah, what the heck? I'll kick him loose.' See, that ain't gonna work with me, but you don't know that. You oughta give it a shot. This whole life is one big con. You gotta learn that. If you don't, you don't survive, kid. That's just how it is." He took another puff on his cigarette, then twisted a little more in his chair so that he was looking at David. "Do you see what I'm telling you?"

"Yes."

"No, you don't. You're just sitting there saying, 'Yes,' because you think that's what I want to hear, but you don't get it. You ain't smart, kid, or at least you ain't learned to play things smart yet. That's why you need to go back home. You just ain't gonna get by any other way."

Suddenly Ralph got up and walked across the lobby. David couldn't see him for quite some time, and he hoped he wouldn't come back, but before long he returned with two suitcases. He set them in the room, close to David, and he tagged them and then left again.

When he came back in a few minutes, he sat down and picked up his cigarette, which was still burning, and he rolled it in his fingers. "Okay," he said, "now right there was a good example. That guy says to me, 'I wanta leave some bags with you. You gonna be here when I get back?' So I says, 'Probably. What time are you coming back?' He says, 'I'm not sure. It could be three or four o'clock.' So I says, 'Well, I'll be gone by then, sir, but another boy will be here. Don't worry about that.' So he says, 'Well, let me take care of you now.' And he hands me a buck. Now—do you see what I did there?"

"No." David felt like saying, "And I don't care either."

"That's right. You don't. But I'm thinking all the time.

64

I see this guy's been around. I know he travels on an expense account. He's got himself a suit that set him back maybe four or five hundred bucks, and he likes to tip, see. That's something you gotta know about a guy. So—if I say, 'Oh, I might not be here when you get back,' he says, 'The guy's trying to con me. Forget it.' But I say I probably will be. That's what I say first, and he figures I'm being straight with him. Then I say, 'Probably not that long, but that's okay.' Now he thinks he ain't been conned, and he's a big shot if he lays a lousy buck on me. He hits me with a dollar, and that ain't much, but it's a dollar I wouldn't have had. See what I did? I conned him by making him think I didn't con him. See what I'm saying to you?"

"Yes."

"No, you don't." Ralph cursed loudly, obviously irritated. "I'll tell you, kid, you don't get anything. You sit there and say you do, but you ain't even listening, not really. I'm just gonna say this, and then I ain't saying nothing else to you. Paul knows how to play the role, like he's the nicest guy around—all that soft talk and everything. But that don't work the way he thinks it does. You could learn a whole lot more from me. I make half my money around here selling city tours. I sell twice as many as Paul does. And that's because I know people. Paul thinks he's too good to hustle a guy for a city tour, but I'm the guy who goes home with the money in my pocket."

Ralph had said his last words. He nodded and pointed at David, and then he walked away. He was only gone a couple of minutes, however, and when he came back, Paul was with him. "No," Ralph was saying. "No way. What

65

I ought to do is fire you right here and now. I can tell you, this is your last warning. This is the worst stunt you've ever pulled."

Paul nodded. He stepped over and patted David on the shoulder. He was moving smoothly, and he spoke softly, carefully. "Ralph, I know I shouldn't have done it. I felt sorry for him. I've been trying to figure something out. But you're right. I never should have let him in the room."

"Paul, how stupid do you think I am? Don't you think I know what kind of manure you're shoveling on me? I just told the kid here about conning people, and now you're trying to work around me. Don't try that stuff with me."

"Well, Ralph, I don't know what you want me to say."

"I don't want you to say nothing. I want you to call the police station—send this boy where he belongs."

"Listen, Ralph, here's what I want to do. I'm due in here at three. It's almost ten now. That gives me some time. I was going to wait until Monday to talk to Arnie. But maybe I can get hold of him now—if I can get his home phone number—and maybe he knows what can be done. I'll be back here for my shift. You let David stay right here, and if I haven't worked anything out, I'll make the phone call. I'll call the cops."

Ralph thought that over. He got out another cigarette and lit it, taking lots of time. "Why should I do that, Paul?" he finally said. "The way I see it, you owe me plenty, and I don't owe you a single favor. You think you're better'n me, and you try to run this place, even though I'm your boss. Now, you tell me why I should do something extra for you."

David saw the flash, saw Paul's jaw tighten and his fingers clench. And then he saw Paul let it go, let loose. "I don't know, Ralph. But I don't think this is a favor for me. I know you're covering for me. You could go ahead and tell Mr. Raymond what I did, and I'd be out the door. In fact, if that's what you feel you gotta do, go ahead. But give me today to see what I can work out for this boy. That's all I'm asking you."

Ralph laughed, sucking air across his tight lip. "Paul, you're something, I'll tell you." Ralph looked at David. "Now, that's what I was talking about, kid. That's a con. It was pretty good, but it won't work. He can't get around me because I know every hustle in the book."

Paul had gone tight again, but he was clenching, holding on. It was David who spoke. "That's okay, Paul. Just call the police. I don't want to get you in trouble."

Ralph laughed in a burst. "Now, that one was not great, but the kid is catching on," he said. "In fact, I'm so glad to see this kid show a little gumption finally, I'm going to bite on that one and play like I don't know it's a con. Get out of here, Paul. Do what you gotta do. But at three, straight up, you have some place for this kid to go, or you make the call to the cops."

Paul said nothing to Ralph for the moment. David knew he was too mad. But he patted David on the shoulder and said, "I'll be back." And then, as he was leaving, he turned and said, "Ralph, don't say anything to Mr. Raymond, all right?"

"No, Paul. Don't worry. I talk to that jerk as little as I can." Ralph laughed. And then he walked out and sat on his chair again. And he talked. He complained about the hotel not being busy, about not making any money, about Paul. "I'll tell you something, kid," he said at one point. "You think calling the cops is a bad deal, but they'll figure out where you're from and take you back, and even though you think you don't want that, it's the best thing. I know about that. I've got six kids of my own. I know something about kids. Do you believe that? Do you believe I got six kids?"

"I don't know."

"Tell the truth. Do you believe it or not? Maybe I'm putting a con on you. What do you think? Do I have six kids?"

"I guess not."

"See, you don't have a feel for this. That time I was telling the truth. I got six kids. Two boys and four girls. Had 'em in nine years. Or my wife did, I didn't." He laughed. "I see 'em all once a month now. That's all. My wife and me, we're separated. We got some things we gotta work out, see, and then I'll probably go back. But I told the woman what I expected, and when it didn't happen, I said, 'All right, then, I'm outa here.'" He slapped the desk with his open hand. "I go up there—up in Lynnwood, north of here—once a month. She begs me every time to come home and stay, but I ain't ready."

That one David wasn't buying. He thought maybe Ralph's wife kicked him out. David was also glad when things got a little busier and Ralph had to leave a good deal. But Ralph was back and forth, and each time he came back he wouldn't stop talking. David tried not to listen, tried to think. As the day wore on, he gradually made up his mind what he had to do. He knew this Arnie guy couldn't solve anything. David just had to get out of the hotel.

The worst thought for David was that he wouldn't see Paul to say good-bye, or Rob and Elaine—or Melissa. He told himself it didn't matter, but it was still what held him back for a while, until he finally decided he just had to get going.

He got his coat, and he stepped to the door. He held the coat behind the door casing. But Ralph was out on the floor. And when Ralph would leave, Betty kept watching, smiling at him when she saw him looking her way. The better part of an hour passed, with David watching for a chance. A couple of times Ralph came back to the desk and talked. David had to step back and put his coat down.

Time was running out, and David knew he had to find his chance. When Ralph finally left the floor again, David decided he couldn't worry about Betty. He walked slowly to the center of the little lobby, carrying his coat, and he said, "Thanks for helping me, but I gotta go now." He started for the door, walking fast.

"No, David," Betty said. He heard the little door swing, the one at the end of the desk. He hurried, pushed through the glass doors, dodged to the left, and took off running. He made it to the corner and made another quick left turn, and then ran straight down the street. He hadn't gone half a block before he saw Paul coming toward him.

He stopped, stood still for a moment, thought about dodging across the street. But he couldn't do it. He couldn't run from Paul, not now that he had seen him.

"David, what are you doing?"

"Paul, thanks. I'm okay now. I'm going."

"Going where?"

"I don't know. California, when I can."

"No, David. I can't let you do that." Paul reached out and put his hand on David's shoulder. "It won't work." He took David by the arm, turned him. "We can figure something out," he said. He began to walk back toward the hotel, not gripping tight but pushing rather firmly. David knew he could pull loose if he tried. And yet, he also knew that he was relieved.

Betty and Ralph were standing at the doors to the hotel. When Paul came in with David, Ralph swore. "Paul, that's stupid," he said. "I just told Betty. Let the kid run. Maybe that's the only way he's going to learn anything. We try to be nice to the little jerk, and he takes off on us. He deserves what he gets."

Paul spun around. "Shut your mouth, Ralph. Okay? Just once, for thirty lousy seconds, shut your mouth."

8

"Don't worry. He won't fire me," Paul said, but David wasn't sure. Ralph had left the hotel cursing and warning, threatening Paul that if he didn't have David out of the hotel in ten minutes he wouldn't have a job.

"You shouldn't have said that to him."

"That's where you're wrong, David. I should have said a whole lot more. I'm sick of the guy." Paul was standing at the bellmen's desk, just outside the room, where Ralph had been before. "The great carney. He never said anything he meant in his whole life. The truth is, he would fire me, but then he'd have to go to all the trouble to find someone else." He leaned against the door frame. "But I'll tell you something. He just might be right about calling the cops. That might be the best thing for you. They would make you go home, and that's where you need to be."

"Don't call 'em, okay?"

Paul walked into the room, stood close to David. "Tell me why not."

David took a breath. Something told him he had to give Paul a little more to go on. Paul had stuck his neck way out for him. "I don't have a home."

"What does that mean?"

But David still didn't want to talk about it. He waited for a time and then finally looked up into Paul's eyes. "I don't have any parents. They got killed in a car wreck."

"Just recently?"

"No. Two years ago. Two years and two months."

"So where have you been living?"

"Different places. Mostly in foster homes."

"Why didn't they just put you with one family and leave you there?"

More than anything else, David didn't want to talk about that. "I don't know."

"Didn't things work out with some of them?"

"No. They didn't."

"Okay. I guess I understand better now. But look, the only thing to do is try again and see if you can't get a nice family this time. I talked to Arnie. He said he should be able to find you a family. I told him I thought you were trying to get away from your own—but this doesn't make a lot of difference. If some foster family hasn't been right with you, I'm sure it's easier to get you away from them than it would be from your real parents."

"I don't want another foster family."

"Why?"

"I just don't."

"That's stupid, David. That's just plain bullheaded and stupid. You're eleven years old, for crying out loud. You can't just roam around for ten years."

"In California I can pick fruit and stuff like that. I already found out about that."

Paul shook his head and laughed. "No. No way. A big kid could maybe get some work. But a little kid like you wouldn't have a chance."

David wouldn't look at Paul. "I'm not going to a foster home again. I don't care what you do. I'll run away again the first time I get a chance."

Paul leaned against the wall. He shrugged and then stuffed his hands into his pockets. "So what do we do?"

"You don't have to do anything. I'll just go."

Paul shook his head slowly, but he said nothing for a long time. David wondered what he was thinking. What he didn't expect was a solution to his problem; there really wasn't one.

"Look," Paul eventually said, "there's a room up on the mezzanine. It used to be a guest room. We just use it for storage now. But there are some mattresses in there. I could get you some blankets, and you could sleep up there tonight."

"You'll get in more trouble."

"No, I won't. No one will know."

"Paul, you just think that if you keep me another day, you can talk me into going to a foster home."

"Yeah, I guess that's what I think. I want you to at least talk to Arnie. He wants you to come over to his office."

"I don't want to talk to him. I know what those guys say. And I know what really happens."

Paul let his breath out in a long gust, and then he nodded. David felt a shaky sense that the end had come. Finally Paul said, "But you might as well sleep here tonight. I don't know what else to tell you."

"Okay. I'll leave in the morning." David knew the real truth. He wanted another night; he was as scared as Paul about going back out into the streets. And he wanted to see Rob and Elaine again.

Paul nodded, as though he accepted the reality. But then the bell rang out front and he said to sit tight for the moment. He walked out to the lobby and was gone for quite a while. When he eventually came back, he had David hurry to the stairway while the desk clerk had stepped away. He took David to the storage room, which wasn't anything David liked very much. There was no TV. There were no lamps, so the only lights were in the entrance and in the bathroom. David really only had a little corner to sit in. Most of the room was full of old furniture. Paul had made a sort of bed on top of a stack of mattresses.

"I'll stop by once in a while," Paul said. "I'll get you some food, too."

David said he would be fine. But when Paul was gone, there was nothing to do. He was relieved not to be out in the cold; and yet, walking the streets, watching TV, doing almost anything would be better than sitting alone in this dark room. For the first time since he had run away he wished he had a place to go back to. He would almost rather go back to the Poulters'. But that was not an option. They had already told him that. The memory of what Mr. Poulter had said struck David, and it hurt all over again.

David didn't want to cry. He had told himself a thousand times that he would never cry again. He had cried every day at first, but crying didn't help. It made things worse. He told himself he could hold out for a few hours. Paul had promised to bring him dinner, and then, after that, he would sleep. And he would get up in the night and go down to the desk. That was something to look forward to. And yet, the tears were coming, running slowly down his cheeks, dripping from his chin. He didn't wipe them away, tried not to acknowledge them, and he bit down on his tongue to make it hurt, to make himself mad. The trouble was, he just couldn't find the anger he wanted—needed.

Paul came by a couple of times, and he brought the food he had promised. He also brought a couple of books he had found somewhere. David ate the meal, but he didn't open the books. He got out his pocketknife and opened the blades and shut them. He was careful with the knife, remembering what Billy had always told him. But the thought of Billy was too much, and the tears came again. He put the knife away and got up on the mattresses. And then he fell asleep.

When he awoke, he had no idea what time it was, but it was still dark. He got down from the mattresses and worked his way through the furniture, over to the window. Across the street he could see the little diner. It was an old-fashioned place, with a counter and some booths.

75

There were a few people inside, but he couldn't see a clock. A woman was sitting in a booth by herself, looking down at a cup of coffee. She was lonely, David thought. He couldn't stand to look at her. He got away from the window.

It could be ten o'clock, or it could be four in the morning. David had no idea, and there was no phone in this room. But he put his shoes on, and then he stepped outside slowly. He had no key, so he didn't pull the door all the way closed.

David had heard noises on the mezzanine earlier, people in some of the reception rooms, but now all was quiet. He sneaked down the stairs, then waited in the dark and looked out across the lobby. He could see Rob, with his head down, working on the audit. Elaine was probably behind the switchboard, but he couldn't see her from where he was.

It would be okay, David decided. He stepped out into the lobby, walked quickly across, without saying anything until he was almost at the desk. But just as he said, "Hi, Rob," he realized that Clark was sitting at the bellmen's desk. He didn't know what Clark would think of this.

"Hey, David," Rob said, "how's my man?"

"Is that my David boy?" Elaine said, in her little voice.

"What are you doing up already?" Rob asked.

"I don't know. What time is it?"

"About twelve." He looked at his watch. "Well, twenty after. That's pretty early to be getting up for the day."

"I went to sleep right after supper," he said.

"Yeah, that's what Paul said. Come around here. I'll open your office." He didn't seem to be concerned about

Clark. Elaine was coming now, meeting David as soon as he came behind the desk. "Oh, honey," she said, crouching down in front of him. "You look so worn out." And then she was hugging him. David stood stiff, not knowing what to do. But she was holding him close, patting his back. When she stepped back, she said, "Now, come here. I've got to have a chat with you."

David followed her to the switchboard. Elaine sat down and then said, "David, honey, you've got to listen to Paul. You need to find a nice family. That's just the only thing to do. Now, why don't you want to do that?"

"I can't," David said, but he wouldn't look at her. He didn't know what Paul had told them. Maybe they knew about his parents. He didn't mind if they did, but he didn't want to tell them himself, didn't want to have to say the words.

"Why not, honey?"

David suddenly wished he hadn't come down. He would not answer. He didn't want to go through this again.

Rob seemed to understand. "Hey, old lady, get off the kid's back, will you? He's got his reasons."

Elaine ignored Rob. She talked to David about his clothes. She told him that she had fixed the jeans she had bought him. She wanted him to change, and she would take home the ones he had on. David didn't have the heart to tell her that he wouldn't be back tomorrow.

"I'll tell you what I think," Rob said, interrupting Elaine. "I think the kid's really a bank robber, disguised as a kid. He's hiding out from the law."

Rob had opened the door to the little office, but he had

set the chair right in the doorway, where David could see, and people could see David. He motioned for David to sit down.

"Okay, tell us the truth. What's your real name? I never knew a bank robber named David. It's always Lefty, or Slim, or Blacky, or something like that."

"Bruno," David said softly. He walked over and sat down. He wanted to start laughing, to get Rob joking around.

"What?"

"Bruno. That's my real name." It was a name David had heard in a movie.

Rob laughed hard, his voice bouncing around in the empty lobby. "Right. Now, that sounds more like it. Bruno fits a bad guy like you better than David."

"I like the name David." David knew the voice. Melissa was coming across the lobby. In a moment he could see her at the desk. She was wearing a pink T-shirt, and she had her hair in a ponytail. She looked really young.

"Melissa," Rob said, "have I ever mentioned that I worship you from the soles of your pretty little feet to the last strand of your gorgeous hair?"

"Rob, I hate to tell you this, but I have ugly feet—long, skinny, bony toes." She looked at David. "Hi," she said.

David said hello, but he was embarrassed.

"Was it busy tonight?" Elaine asked. She got up from her chair and came to the other end of the desk, where Melissa was.

"No way. The place was dead all night. It always is on Sundays. I don't even know why we open Sunday nights."

"Business people who get in on Sunday afternoon want some place to hang out," Elaine said. "That's what Mr. Raymond says."

"Well, we could close by eight, or at least ten. I don't know why we have to stay open until midnight." She slid her hands into her front pockets. "I'll tell you the truth. I'll never get over feeling guilty about working on Sundays—especially in a bar. My parents would die if they knew. In my home, Sunday was the Sabbath. We went to church. My dad wouldn't even work in the yard that day."

"Tell the truth," Rob said. "You hate working down there every day—not just on Sunday."

"True," Melissa said. "At night, I walk out of here and breathe that cold air and I feel like a human being again. Some days I go sit in the park all afternoon, just to smell something that's alive."

"You ought to get out of there," Elaine said. "I wonder if the hotel wouldn't give you a job out here on the desk. Maybe you should put in for that."

"No chance, Elaine. I didn't even graduate from high school. They'd never let me work on the desk. I don't know if I'd like it anyway."

"I don't see what difference a year or two of school would make. You could handle all this okay. And I know you'd like it. People are nice around a hotel. Most of the guests are nice as they can be."

Rob laughed. "Elaine thinks everyone's nice."

"No, I don't. But most people are."

From across the lobby, Clark said, "I'll tell you a story about Elaine." He got up and walked over to the desk. He was sort of half smiling. "We had a couple check in here one night. From Texas. They went down to the bar and had a few drinks—quite a few—and they got in a big fight." Clark stopped and chuckled to himself. "So the two of them got on the elevator and went upstairs. They were staying on the twentieth floor—the very top of the hotel. I guess they kept the fight going, and the guy finally said he was leaving. He got his bags all packed up and he was about to walk out. Do you remember this, Elaine?"

Elaine was grinning. "Sure I do. But it was fifteen years ago, at least."

"So anyway, we heard this big crash and we weren't sure exactly where it come from. In a minute, this Texan comes down the elevator and says his wife threw his suitcase out the window. We went outside to the parking lot, and that bag—one of those big, old Samsonites—had gone right through the roof of a car out here behind the hotel. I mean, smashed right through it. The guy was still sort of drunk, and he was so mad he started screaming that he was going to go upstairs and throw his wife out the window. Well, Elaine kind of pats him on the shoulder, and she says, 'I wouldn't do that. What if you smashed another car? Then you'd have two to pay for.' Well, this old boy from Texas, richer than a skunk, he starts to laugh, and he says, 'That wouldn't be too smart, would it?' And off he goes to the elevator, laughing all the way. The next day that pair checked out of the hotel, and they were hanging all over each other, like they were on their honeymoon."

Everyone laughed, and Clark was still chuckling to himself. "Elaine always knows the right thing to say. That's how she's always been."

Melissa was smiling, looking at Elaine. "I didn't know you'd worked here that long," she said.

"Longer than that. It'll be twenty-two years this next spring."

"Is that when your husband died?"

"No. He died long before that."

"What happened to him? How did he die?"

David saw Rob slide his hands into his pockets and look down. But Elaine said, quietly, "He did something stupid. He went out fishing, all by himself, and somehow he tipped over the boat. He was out on Lake Washington and it wasn't windy or anything. But he tipped over the little boat, and the police figured he tried to swim for it instead of hanging on and waiting. Which was just like him. The guy never had an ounce of patience in him."

"How old was he?"

"He was going to turn twenty-three, just the week after."

"Didn't you have any children?"

"Yes. I had a little girl. Louise was her name. Not quite a year after her daddy died, she got pneumonia, and she died, too. Back in those days, they just couldn't do much when a little one got that sick."

"Oh, Elaine, that must have been so awful," Melissa said.

Elaine nodded; she looked down at her hands, lying in her lap. She ran a finger along a bulging blue vein on the back of one hand. "She was only two. I'd had her long enough to be used to her, you know. And after her daddy died, she was the only thing I had. I guess I spoiled her. But I loved her so much."

David saw the tears in Elaine's eyes.

"It's been forty-six years. I ought to be over it by now."

"Some things just keep hurting," Melissa said, and she looked down at the desk. No one spoke.

David knew what Melissa meant. He thought of his parents' funeral—the stupid funeral, when no one came. His mother's two sisters and one neighbor. And the minister saying that everything was okay. But David knew he shouldn't think about that. He bit down on his tongue, bit harder this time.

Melissa was watching David. He wouldn't look back at her, but he kept catching little glimpses. Finally she said, "David, tell us something about you. We've all told you something about us."

David looked at the cabinets under the front desk, ran his eyes over the grain in the wood. He had a feeling that it would be a mistake to tell them, and yet, he wanted them to know. "Two years ago my family got in a bad car wreck. I got hurt pretty bad. But my mom and dad got killed, and so did my big brother."

"Oh, David," Melissa said.

Elaine came to him and put her arm around his shoulders. "Paul already told us—Rob and me," she said. "I'm sorry, David."

"I'm okay now," David said. "It was a long time ago." He wouldn't cry, he told himself.

A hard time followed—silence—and David knew they were all looking at him. Rob tried to change the subject, but no one really said very much. Melissa finally said she had to go home, but first she came behind the desk to David. "I'm sorry," she said, and she patted him on the head. "You remind me of my little brother. I haven't seen him for a long time, so I guess he's grown up a lot. But you remind me of the way he was. And I miss him."

At five-thirty David went back to the storage room. He looked through the books for a while and then put them down. He sat on the floor, leaning against the wall, and he stared ahead. At the time he hadn't regretted telling them. He liked the way they had all treated him. But now what? He would have to leave them, and then he would only be worse off. He hadn't wanted ever to lose anyone again. Suddenly he was mad at himself. Why had he said anything? It only made things ten times worse. He saw a vision of the next morning, saw himself walking, heading away from the hotel, and he saw blackness, like a cave, before him, and nothing else.

He curled up on the floor, not exactly intending to sleep, but trying hard not to think, not to see the blackness. When he woke up, Paul was whispering to him, "Hey, partner, why didn't you get up on the mattresses?"

David sat up and rubbed his face with the palms of his hands. He was tired and confused, and his face felt dry, almost brittle. He remembered what he had been feeling when he went to sleep, but somehow it all seemed different now. He wasn't sure what to feel. He kept wanting to hope for something, and yet he knew he shouldn't do that.

Paul sat down on the floor. He had a white paper bag with him. "I brought you something to eat. I had to come into the hotel through the kitchen and sneak around Ralph. I hope you don't mind a hamburger for breakfast."

"What time is it?"

"Nine-thirty. You're so messed up on your sleep, you may never get straight again. Did you go down with Rob and Elaine again?"

"Yeah. And Melissa."

"Melissa? Do you know her, too?"

"Yeah. I met her before."

"She's some fine-looking woman, isn't she?"

"She's nice," David said, almost in her defense.

"Yes, she is nice. Guys who just see her down in the lounge don't know that." Paul leaned back against the wall. "She's real quality, too."

"Why don't you marry her?"

"Marry her?" Paul laughed. "Oh, yeah, I can just see that."

"No, really. Why don't you?"

"Well, first, I don't plan on getting married. Second, I'm twice her age. And third, she knows about me."

"Knows what?"

Paul leaned his head back against the wall, looked off over David's head. He was wearing the gray jacket again and the black shirt. He looked handsome, but he also looked tired. There was a hint of yellowness in his eyes and skin, and circles under his eyes. "You know. About my drinking."

"You don't drink anymore."

"Not lately. But people know how drunks are. They figure I'll fall off the wagon one of these days. They might be right, too."

"That's why you should get married."

"You think that's the answer, huh?" He smiled, still looking off in the distance.

"When I had a family, things were okay," David said. "Better than now anyway."

Paul looked at David. "Yeah, well, I'm sure that's true. But my situation is a little different." He handed David the sack. "You better eat this," he said.

David opened the sack and found a big hamburger, fries, and a Coke. "Thanks," he said, and got the hamburger out.

"I've been married three times already," Paul said, "and I messed up every time."

"How'd you mess up?"

"Drinking, of course. Running around. My wives were married to me, but I wasn't married to them. I was too busy living the fast life with all my buddies—and with other women, too."

"You wouldn't do that now."

"Maybe." Paul pulled his knees up and rested his arms on them. "I have three kids, David. Three daughters. I had two with my first wife and one with my second. But I'm not even sure where they are now. I can imagine what they must think of me. If they remember me at all, they remember some drunk slapping their mother around."

David wasn't exactly surprised. He had seen some of Paul's anger. And yet, he didn't want to believe it. "Did you ever hit your kids?"

"Yeah. Not real bad. Not the way my dad did to me. But bad enough."

"But you don't drink now. You wouldn't do that."

"I don't know." David saw the sadness in Paul's eyes again. He thought he understood it better now. "Well, anyway," Paul said, "I don't know why we're talking about me. You're the one who needs a family. Maybe you can get married. You probably have a better chance with Melissa than I do."

"I don't think so. She says I remind her of her little brother." David smiled, but he was embarrassed. He could feel that he was blushing.

"Well, you need to grow a couple of feet taller. Do you think you could manage that in the next few days?"

"I'll try." It was the first time he had admitted it to himself, but he knew that was exactly what he wished he could do.

Paul looked at David for some time, smiling. "You're some kid," he said. "It turns out, you can even talk."

"My mom used to say I never stopped talking."

"Your real mom?"

David paused, and then he nodded.

"You miss her, don't you?"

"Sure, who wouldn't?" he said. He was suddenly irritated, mostly with himself. Why had he done this again?

"Well, listen, partner, we've got to get you out of here. No one ever comes in this room at night. But during the day, you never know."

David looked over at his coat. Paul noticed. "Are you ready to go talk to Arnie?" he asked.

"No."

"Come on, David. Let's not go through this again. It can't hurt to talk to him. I'll go with you, and we'll explain everything. Let's at least see what the options are."

"I'm not going down there, Paul," David said. "I'm leaving now." He got up.

Paul was still sitting on the floor. "I could force you to go with me," he said. David heard the frustration, the flash of anger. "That's just exactly what I ought to do, too. There's no talking any sense into you."

David got his coat and put it on. He hated this tone. Adults always came around to it sooner or later. They were always so sure they knew what was best. But David had seen what adults could do for him.

"David, you're thinking about this all wrong. It seems to me like you've gotta keep trying no matter what has happened to you before. You're too young to give up on everybody."

"You should talk."

"What do you mean by that?"

"You aren't trying anymore. You just said that."

"That's not what I said. I told you I had my chance and I messed things up. You're quitting before you even try."

"I'm not quitting. I'm just not going back to any more families. You're the one who's quitting."

"No. No way. When I quit, I'll go get good and drunk. I haven't done that yet."

"That's just so you won't die."

"Sure it is. And as long as I keep staying alive, I haven't quit."

"Everybody's afraid to die. That's nothing to brag

88

about." David hardly knew what he was saying. He just knew he was mad or that he wanted to be. And suddenly he wanted to hate Paul. He wanted to walk away, turn his back and go—and he wanted to feel nothing but anger. He could even face the darkness if he was mad enough.

Paul got up. He pointed a finger in David's face. "Don't talk to me about things you don't understand. You're in no position to start telling me how I ought to live my life. You're the kid who's running away. I don't know what makes you think you've got a lot to be proud of."

David zipped up his coat. "Maybe I don't," he said. "But when I get grown up I'm going to get married, and I'm going to have some kids, and I'm going to come home after work and play baseball with 'em. I'm not going to beat up on anybody." David half expected Paul's fist, half wanted it. But his stomach muscles were quivering, his chest tightening up.

Paul was staring at him. "You don't know that, David. You don't know what you'll do. Nobody expects to mess up. When my old man used to slug me, I swore I'd never treat a kid like that. And then I turned out to be a lousy father, too. Maybe I was worse—because I took off—and at least he stuck around. Maybe that's what you'll do, too—just keep running away all the time."

"You don't know what you're talking about, Paul. You don't know what I've done. You don't know how many families I've been with. You don't know if I've tried or not."

"That's right. Because you won't tell me. You clam up every time I try to find out anything about you. You don't trust me, David. You don't trust anybody."

"I don't have to tell you anything. Why should I?"

"Because by now you ought to be able to see that I'm not trying to get anything from you. I happen to be trying to help you."

"So I guess it's time I'm supposed to tell you thanks again so you can feel like some kind of big hero. Well, thanks two million this time. Now, how do I get out of here?"

Paul didn't move for a long time, except that he was breathing deep, his chest swelling and releasing in a slow rhythm. David knew he was trying to keep control, trying to think what to do.

"David, all that stuff Ralph says—all that crap about everybody conning everybody. That isn't right. There's a lot of it that goes on. But you have to play it straight with somebody sooner or later. Do you know what I'm talking about?"

"No."

"I don't believe that. You know exactly what I'm talking about. There's just a time when you have to trust somebody. You can't make up your mind, like Ralph does, that everybody's out to get you."

"I've trusted people. You don't know what I've done. You don't know what happened either."

"Tell me about it. Let's talk. Let's see what we can—"

"I gotta go, Paul. I'll find the way."

"Okay." The word came with force, this time without control. "Fine. You get your little fanny out on the street and see how you like it. There's no getting through to you.

I guess somebody really messed you up, and maybe that's not your fault, but there's not one damn thing I can do about it—because you won't let me."

Paul took the lead, guided David down to the kitchen and out a back door into the hotel parking lot. David hadn't known exactly what he was pushing for, but this wasn't it. He felt a kind of panic, a desperation, and yet he had no idea what he could do about it now. As he stepped outside, he felt the wind. It wasn't raining, but the air was damp and cold. He was terrified now that he faced it—much more frightened than when he had left the Poulters. He even knew why, but he couldn't say it to himself.

Paul turned around. He didn't look angry now—that had already passed—but his eyes were cold. "Where are you going to go?" he asked.

"I don't know. I'll figure something out."

"Oh, man." Paul put his hands on his hips and stared over David's head. "This is *stupid*. There's no reason for this. There's not one reason in the world for a kid like you to be wandering around when he could have a home." He looked up at the dreary sky.

David waited. He wondered what Paul was thinking. And then he admitted to himself what he hoped, what he wanted Paul to say.

"Look at this weather, David. How are you going to stay warm tonight?"

David didn't answer. He didn't know.

"What can be so bad about going over to talk to Arnie?"

Those weren't the words David needed. Paul still didn't understand.

"Look," Paul said, but then he hesitated. David held his breath. "Why don't you do this? Walk around for a few hours. Get some exercise. Go in some stores to keep warm. And then come back here this afternoon when I'm back on shift. You can sleep in the storage room again tonight."

"I don't want to do that."

"Why not?"

"You just keep saying to stay another day, another day. But it doesn't do any good."

"I know. But you won't do what you've gotta do. And I can't think of one thing to tell you. All I know is that I don't want you to sleep outside tonight, and I can't think of any other place to put you."

David looked down. It wasn't going to happen. He had been stupid even to think about it. He needed the anger now, and it was failing him.

"Will you do that?"

"No."

"Come back about four or so. Ralph will be long gone by then. Just come to this door and wait outside until I come out and get you."

David shook his head, didn't look at Paul.

"If I don't know where you are tonight, I'll be sick wondering about you." Slowly Paul's hand came up and rested on David's head, lightly. "David, I just can't let you wander off like this."

He hadn't said it—not what David wanted—but it was

close, and something released in David's chest. He wanted more than anything to grab Paul, to cling to him.

"Will you do that, David? Will you come back here this afternoon?"

David looked up for just a moment. He was embarrassed, and he knew Paul was, too. "Okay," he whispered.

Paul nodded. "I'll meet you right here. Four o'clock."

David nodded, too, and then he walked away without looking up into Paul's face again.

10

David walked. He was not cold once he got moving, and he actually enjoyed being outside. He walked all the way out to the Space Needle and back to town, and he strolled through a couple of downtown department stores. He had no idea what good it would do to go back to the hotel another night. It was only one more delay, probably bound to make things even worse. And yet, he kept feeling a vague comfort in what Paul had said, and in spite of himself, he couldn't resist a sense of hope.

That afternoon, when he showed up at the hotel, Paul was waiting. He said, "Good. I'm glad you came back." David saw the relief in Paul's face. "I'm going to take you up to a guest room for a little while, where you can watch some TV, and then you'll have to go back to the storage room to sleep."

David was glad to have a television set again. He didn't

get in bed. Paul had said not to. He wasn't tired anyway. He watched a movie until he decided he didn't like it, and then he switched channels for a while until he found a sitcom he sort of liked.

Paul came by with food, and then a little later he came into the room looking rather rushed. "Okay, partner," he said, "we've got a bit of a problem. Get your shoes on."

Paul went to the telephone and dialed. "Howard?" he said. "Hey, I don't see any problem with this room. It must have been flagged by mistake. It looks like someone came back in after it was made up—maybe used the toilet—but a maid could fix it up in five minutes and you could use it."

Paul put the phone down. "The hotel's getting busier. Howard needs some rooms. He's the guy on the desk in the evenings. He's not the kind of guy who would go along with all this the way Rob does. Come with me. Bring your coat."

David followed Paul to the elevator. "I can't take you back to that storage room. Not yet. There's a reception or party or something on the mezzanine. I can't get you into that room without a lot of people seeing us."

David was scared. But it was for Paul, not for himself.

"Stand over there," Paul said. "I'll make sure there's no one on the elevator. He had a set of keys in his hand. As soon as the elevator opened, he nodded to David and they both got on. Paul used the key to turn a switch. "Now the elevator won't stop for anyone," he said.

When the elevator stopped and the door opened, David could see that they were in the basement. "Okay," Paul

95

said, "go over there in the corner. Sit down back by those rolled-up carpets. It'll be dark once this door shuts. If anyone comes down here, just sit still. But no one will. I'll be back for you in a few minutes."

David did as he was told. But as the door shut, the darkness was complete. David felt nervous and terribly alone. It made him think of the nights he had spent outside.

Ten minutes went by, and David's eyes never adjusted enough for him to see much of anything. When he heard footsteps, his breath caught and suddenly he could hear his own heart beating.

"David?"

"Yeah."

"I came down the stairs. I don't know where the light switch is. Just come to my voice. Can you see?"

"No." But David was up and moving toward the voice.

"Okay, keep coming. Get hold of my coat. We'll go upstairs, and then I want you to stand in the stairwell until I come and tell you it's clear out front. I'll sneak you into the bellmen's room. You'll be okay there for a while."

When Paul walked out into the lobby, David was left in the dark again. He stood against the wall, wondering whether someone might come up or down the stairs. It didn't seem to be a set of stairs that hotel guests used, but he wasn't sure.

Paul was back quickly this time. "Okay, hurry," he said. "Howard just stepped into the back room." The two walked quickly into the lobby, a few steps over to the bellmen's desk, and then into the bellmen's room. Paul had left the door open.

"Okay, you're all right now. Just stay back where no one can see you, even when the door opens. I'll come in once in a while to keep you company, but it's kind of busy tonight, so I might be gone quite a bit. Maybe you can read those books I got you. They're right there on that shelf."

He was gone again. David was still nervous. He knew Paul was taking a big chance.

Paul came in lots of times during the evening, sometimes staying a few minutes. Only later on in the shift, however, did things slow down enough that he could actually keep David company for a while.

"Are you making lots of money tonight?" David asked, when they had a little time to talk.

"I'm not doing too bad," Paul said.

"How much money do people give you?"

"It depends."

"On what?"

"The people. The Jefferson's a nice little house in some ways. It's small, with not too many rooms on the floors, so a guy can get back to the elevator and down fast. One or two boys can handle it all the time. So that means a guy stays busy when the hotel is busy. Only thing is, we don't get the kind of people in here who tip a whole lot."

"Not enough rich people, I guess."

Paul laughed. "Rich people aren't always the biggest tippers," he said. "It's people who want you to think they're rich that throw the bucks around." Paul had been holding the door slightly open, and he was looking out to the lobby, not at David. But now he turned around. "I'll tell you something, David. People don't tip bellboys.

97

They tip themselves. They give a couple of dollars to a bellboy and then feel good about themselves. For five bucks they can think they're real hot shots. That's not a bad price. Pay five bucks and you're somebody."

"How come it makes you mad?"

"It doesn't make me mad."

"You sound mad."

Paul shrugged, and then he leaned back against the wall. "There's another part to it, David. Once they give me that five bucks, they think they own me. I'm the one who's supposed to fall all over the guy every time he walks through the lobby. I'm the one who's supposed to tell the guy he's a big deal. Maybe that's buying a little too much with a lousy five-dollar bill."

Paul turned, took another look into the lobby, and then he looked at David again. "There's only one way to beat guys like that. Maybe I'm only a bellboy, but I make those guys feel like I have about six times more class than they do. I tell them—without saying it—that they don't have enough bills in their wallets to buy me."

"How do you do that?"

"I don't know. There's a way. It's style, or something. It's the way you handle yourself. Ralph hustles people. They see through him, and they hate him for it. He comes down that elevator with change in his pockets. I don't sell that cheap. Nobody gives me their small change. It would make them feel stupid to do that to me."

David thought of the smoothness. Maybe he understood it now. "Don't you like the people who tip you?" he asked.

"It's not that." But Paul couldn't look at David. "Some of the people are really . . ." He stopped, and he shoved his hands into his pockets. His eyes came back up slowly. "No. I guess I don't like any of them. I guess I've been mad my whole life that I have to hop around for people, but it's just lately that I finally figured that out. Ralph thinks he's a con man. I am one."

"That's not true, Paul."

"You don't know me, David. Not really."

"I think I do."

Paul smiled, but not with any joy. "You only know one side of me. You don't know what I can be like. I guess I've got a lot of hate stored up—and sometimes it all busts out."

"When you drink?"

"Yeah, mostly when I drink."

"But you don't drink anymore."

"That doesn't make the hate go away."

David didn't know how to talk about this. He just knew that Paul was being too hard on himself.

"David, I've been in jail. I got fired from a hotel in Vegas—because I showed up drunk. I beat up on the bell captain, right there in the lobby of the hotel. It took two cops to pull me off him. Do you see what I'm telling you? I'm not anyone you can . . . rely on. You can't start thinking that I am."

Suddenly David knew what they were talking about. In a strange way, he was relieved. At least Paul knew what David wanted.

"I live in a dump, David. I'm a drunk. I lose my temper.

I run out on people." Paul pounded his finger against his chest. "You've just got to understand that—and get anything else out of your head."

"I didn't ask you for anything," David said softly, without anger. He looked down at the floor. He knew he was lying, and so did Paul. But they didn't say so.

"Look, I'm doing okay right now. I like this little house. I like the people who work here. I don't pal around with them or anything, but I feel comfortable with them. I guess I'm getting old or something, but I think maybe I'm getting on top of some of this stuff. At least I'm not drinking. But I can't be sure what's going to happen. I can't be sure I've changed all that much. You can understand that, can't you?"

David didn't know the answer to that question. Maybe he could understand. But it didn't matter. The results were the same whether he could or not. The blackness was out there again, waiting for him.

"It always comes around to the same thing, David. We've got to go see Arnie tomorrow."

David was still looking at the floor. "No," he whispered.

Paul didn't argue, and in a few minutes he had to leave.

When it was almost eleven, Rob showed up. David couldn't see him, but he could hear his loud voice out at the desk. Clark came along, too. David heard him talk to Paul outside the room, heard Paul say that David was only staying one more night, and then heard him say, "I know, Clark. It wasn't the sort of thing I'd usually do. We'll get him out tomorrow. Just don't say anything to Ralph, all right?"

Clark came into the bellmen's room. He said hello to David, and he shut the door and started changing clothes. David looked away. "I was sorry to hear what happened to your folks," Clark said. "My daddy died when I was younger than you. But I had a mother. So it wasn't so bad on me as I guess it is on you."

David didn't know what to say.

"My wife died six years ago, and that was worse. I've missed her more than I ever did my daddy."

"I guess you would," David said.

"I'll tell you something, David." He pulled his bellboy trousers up over one skinny white leg and then the other. He was turned away from David, talking toward his locker. "It happened early to you. But it happens to us all. We all gotta say good-bye all the time. When you get my age, everyone starts to go. I've had two brothers and a sister die in the last two and half years. I had a good friend over at the apartment house where I live. We used to play a lot of cards together. He died six weeks ago."

Clark cinched up his belt and turned around. "That's how it is. People die. People go away. That's why it ain't no good to run away. Then you're just bringing things on yourself. I know things might be pretty bad where you were, but you ought to go back. Don't you think?"

"I can't."

Clark nodded. He pulled on his jacket and walked to the mirror. He hooked a little brown bow tie to his shirt collar. "Well, I don't know all about it. I shouldn't say anything. But running sure ain't good." He stepped toward the door. "Anyhow, good luck to you."

David said thanks. Clark opened the door, and when he

did, a man stepped in. "Hi, Clark, where's Paul?"

"On the floor, I guess. Or upstairs."

But the man had seen David now. "Who's this?" he said, smiling, but looking surprised.

Clark hesitated, and then David heard Paul, from outside. "Oh, Howard, the boy's with me. I told him he could wait in there. He's waiting . . . for his family."

"Why didn't you have him sit in the lobby, instead of back in this miserable old room?"

"Oh, uh . . . well, his family didn't want him sitting around by himself. They asked me to keep track of him."

Howard nodded, but he glanced back at David one more time, and David saw that he was less than pleased.

When he walked out, Paul stepped in and shut the door, and then he swore. "I should have thought of something better to say. I couldn't think of anything."

"Will you get in trouble?"

"No. He won't even think about it by tomorrow." But David could see that he was concerned. "Rob and Elaine are here. They said to send you out, so you won't have to sit back here. If you want to sleep, they're going to make you a bed on the floor, in the assistant manager's office."

David followed Paul across the lobby. Howard had left by now and David went behind the desk and said hello to Rob and Elaine. Rob said, "Hey, boy, are you still around here? Can't we get rid of you?"

"You be quiet, Rob," Elaine said. "He's my boy."

"Try grandson, maybe. Or great-grandson."

"That's okay. I'll be his grandma. David, would you like to be my grandson?"

David smiled and nodded.

"See. He loves me. I'm nice to him. I'm not like you."

"Hey, what are you talking about?" Rob said. He looked at Paul. "This crazy old lady gets things mixed up. I buy the boy pie every night. The woman never even offers to chip in a dollar once in a while."

"Oh, you big fibber."

"Well, then, maybe you can be his grandpa," Paul said.

Elaine laughed, but Rob acted offended. "Come off it. That'd marry me off to Elaine. I'm the boy's big brother. You can be his dad. We'll let Clark be the grandpa."

"David thinks I ought to marry Melissa. That'd be okay with me. She could be his mama."

"Yeah, we'd make some family, wouldn't we?" Elaine said. "We're all a bunch of loners. Not one of us knows how to live with anyone else."

"I guess that's right." Paul sounded too serious, and an awkward sort of silence set in until Paul said he had to go. "Maybe David ought to stay back in the office out of sight."

"Don't worry, we'll take care of him," Rob said, and David got ready to go into the office. But just then he saw Melissa coming from across the lobby. She was carrying a tray, and she was wearing her short little waitress uniform. Her shoulders were all bare, and the front of the dress was really low. David was embarrassed to see her that way.

"Hi, David," she said, and then to Paul, "He's my friend, too, now. Did you know that?"

"No, no," Rob said. "You're more than friends. We've already got it all figured out. We're his family. Elaine and

Clark are grandma and grandpa. I'm the big brother. Paul's the daddy and you're the mama. I would gladly change with Paul, of course, but I'm not sure I want to have a kid quite so quick."

"That would be okay, I guess." Melissa put her arm around Paul's shoulder. "I could marry this handsome guy. But I'm too young to have an eleven-year-old boy. I better be the big sister. Maybe Betty can be his mama."

And so it was settled. The family was all arranged. Everyone was looking at David, smiling and seeming quite satisfied. But David couldn't look at any of them for very long. He thought they might see right through him and know how much he wished it were true.

11

"Melissa, maybe you can help us with something," Elaine said. She took off her headset and walked over closer to David. "Paul wants to go see Arnie over at Social Services and see if they can't find David a place to live. But David says he doesn't want to go. Somehow we've got to convince him to change his mind." She put an arm around David's shoulder. "He likes you. Maybe you can help us."

This all came as a surprise to David. Obviously Paul had been talking to Rob and Elaine.

Melissa put her elbow on the desk and leaned over, placing her chin on her hand. She was smiling just a little. David was embarrassed to look at her. "Why don't you want to do that?" David looked at the floor.

"That's what he won't tell us," Elaine said.

"Then he must have a good reason," Melissa said. She

waited until David finally looked at her. "Do you want to come home with me, little brother?" she asked.

David was stunned. The idea was sort of scary. He felt too shy around Melissa, and it was not something he had thought of. And yet, he knew instantly that he would go.

"Could you do that, Melissa?" Paul asked.

"Sure. For a little while. I don't have a bed for him. But he could sleep on my couch."

"He needs to get back in school," Elaine said.

"I know," Melissa said softly. "But maybe he needs a couple of days right now—for himself—before he's ready to do that again."

David felt a strange sensation as he watched Paul. The man was too pleased, too relieved by this. And yet, David was relieved, too. He was glad to have a place to go, not to have to face the streets the next morning.

David stayed with Elaine and Rob for a couple of hours. Just a few minutes after one o'clock, when Melissa got off work, she came up from the bar dressed in jeans and her dark blue jacket. She stood in front of him smiling, her eyes looking navy blue, and the dimple by her mouth showing. David wished she weren't quite so pretty. She made him nervous. "You ready to go?" she asked.

David got his coat and the books Paul had given him and then walked back across the lobby to the desk. "You'll come and see us again, won't you?" Elaine said.

"I guess so."

Rob laughed. "Sure he will. The kid is hooked on our pie. He won't be able to sleep at night if he can't get any."

"Good-bye," David said. He suspected he wouldn't

ever see them again either. Rob reached across the desk and shook David's hand. Elaine had him take the clothes she had bought for him. She came out from behind the desk, hugged him, and kissed him on the cheek.

In the car, with Melissa, he was still at a loss for words. She commented on the weather, told him a little about her apartment on Capitol Hill, talked about what a nice person Elaine was—but David said almost nothing. He sat in the seat, looking ahead at the Seattle night. It had begun to rain and the windshield wipers were swishing back and forth before him. He looked at the wet streets, the reflecting lights on the pavement, and as often as he dared, he glanced at Melissa.

At the apartment, Melissa parked in back and then led David around to the front door. She opened the downstairs door with a key and then walked up to the second floor. The place was old, but clean and well kept. When Melissa unlocked the apartment door and went inside, David stepped in and shut the door behind him, but he stayed where he was. Melissa walked over and turned on a lamp, and then she turned around. "Take off your coat," she said. "Would you like some hot chocolate before we make a bed up for you?"

David shrugged. "That's okay," he said.

"What's okay? To have it or not to have it?" She slipped off her jacket and tossed it on a chair. "I'm having some hot chocolate. I always do. Are you having some with me?"

David nodded.

She laughed. "David, you've got to stop being shy

around me. Now, take off your coat and toss it some-where. I'm not a fussy housekeeper." But the truth was, nothing was out of place.

David slipped off his coat, and he followed Melissa to her kitchen. She got out some milk and poured it in a pan, and she set the pan on her stove and turned on a heating unit. "Sit down, David," she said, and motioned to the kitchen table. There were only two chairs at a little pine table. David slipped into one of the chairs, and she sat down on the other side. The kitchen was bright, with little blue and yellow flowers in the wallpaper, but the walls were bare of anything else. The living room was the same way. It struck David that she hadn't been there long, or that she wasn't intending to stay long.

"Do you like hot chocolate?"

"Sure."

"I like anything chocolate. Mom used to tell me I was going to get pimples when I was a teenager. But I was lucky. I never did. And I ate more chocolate than any-body."

David nodded.

Melissa smiled. "Okay. Tell me some more about you. What's your favorite thing to do? Do you play sports?"

"Not very well."

"What do you like to do then?"

David had to think. "I like movies," he finally said.

"What kind do you like best?"

"Stuff about space and rockets—any kind of exciting stuff."

"When I was your age, just about the only thing I had

to do was go to movies. We only had one theater in our town, but I hardly ever missed a show that came to it. Me and my friend Connie. And we loved love stories. Oh, man, I would sit there and fall in love with all the movie stars, and that's the only thing I could think about. Someday I was going to find some big hunk of a guy like that, and I was going to marry him and be happy forever. That's all there was to life, I thought. Things sure don't turn out the way you think they will."

"Why don't you get married again?"

"Well, I'll tell you. There aren't a lot of movie stars out there. But there are a lot of jerks. I don't seem to meet anyone who's—you know—just nice. Someone who treats me right. But then, how would I? I'm in that bar every night, just keeping away from all the guys who try to grab at me."

"Why don't you get a different job?"

"That's not so easy either. I can probably make more money as a cocktail waitress than just about anything. I don't like it, but I don't know what else I could do."

"Why don't you go back home?"

"To Minnesota?"

"Yeah."

"I don't know." She looked down at the table. David watched her eyelids close for a moment. Her skin looked nice, really soft, in this clear light, and her hair was picking up the light, shining. He was amazed that he was talking so easily with someone so beautiful. "I would like to sometimes. But I probably wouldn't fit in anymore."

"How come?"

"Well, I've . . . been gone quite a while. But let's not talk about me. We were going to talk about you." She leaned over with both elbows on the table. "What else do you like to do?"

"I don't know. When my brother was alive, we walked to the beach sometimes. On Saturdays, Mom would let us go down there almost all day. One time we built a castle taller than me, with cannons and a moat and all that stuff."

"You miss him, don't you?"

"Yeah." For a moment he thought he wanted to change the subject, but then he slid out of his seat, pulled the pocketknife from his pocket, and set it on the table in front of Melissa. "This was his. It was in his pocket when he got killed in the wreck. They gave it to me."

Melissa picked it up, ran her finger along the smooth side. She seemed to understand, but she didn't say anything. She looked up and smiled after a moment, and when she put the knife back in David's hand, she patted his arm. "It sounds like you had a nice family."

David shrugged, and he sat down again. "Things were bad sometimes. My dad was out of work a lot. And he was mad a lot, too. He yelled at my brother all the time."

"Not at you?"

"Mostly at my brother. And my mom."

"Why not you?"

"I don't know. I guess Billy did more stuff that made him mad."

"Was Billy nice to you?"

"Sometimes."

"How much older was he?"

"Three years."

"You don't like to talk about him, do you?"

"I don't know. I guess not."

"Okay." Melissa got up. She stuck a finger in the milk to check it. Then she sucked her finger. "It's not quite ready," she said. "I like it good and hot."

"One thing I like to do is go to the zoo," David said.

"Oh, yeah? Hey, me, too. I love zoos. When I was a kid that was just about the biggest thing in the world. One time we took a trip all the way to southern California. We went to Disneyland, and we went down to the San Diego Zoo. Have you ever heard of that?"

David shook his head.

"Well, it's about the biggest zoo in the world, I guess. I loved it. We were there all day long, and I still didn't want to leave."

"Yeah, me, too. My dad would always want to stay about an hour, and then he'd start saying, 'Come on, let's go. We've been here long enough.' But me and Billy wanted to see everything."

"Where was that? Here at the Seattle Zoo?"

David hesitated, and then he nodded.

"Hey, you know what? I've never been out there. Do you want to go tomorrow? You can show me around."

"Okay. I'll take you to the snakes first."

"Oh, yuck. Forget it. I hate snakes."

David laughed. "That's what my mom always said. She wouldn't even look at snakes. She'd wait outside, and me and Billy would go in there and stay as long as we could."

"What did she like?"

"I don't know. The monkeys. Just about everything."
But all the images were coming back, and suddenly David
knew he couldn't do this anymore. He never seemed to
learn.

"Okay, this milk is ready." She took the pan off the
stove. David watched her pour it in the cups and mix up
the chocolate. Then she brought the cups to the table.
David had to wait to drink his for a time, but Melissa
spooned hers out, blew on it, and then slurped it, making
lots of noise. "If you don't make noise drinking hot chocolate, you aren't doing it right," she said.

So David slurped his, and they both laughed. "You're
teaching me bad habits," David said.

"No way. Hot-chocolate slurping is perfectly proper.
At all the fanciest restaurants, that's how the rich people
drink it."

"Now you're telling lies to a kid. That's even worse.
You could get in a lot of trouble for messing up a poor
little kid like me."

She reached across the table and messed up his hair.
"Ah, David. No one could mess you up. You're too nice.
I didn't know they made kids like you anymore."

David knew she was only kidding around, but he was
still amazed. He didn't know whether he was nice or not.
It had never occurred to him that he was. But Paul had said
it, and Elaine, too, and now Melissa.

"Aren't you getting tired?"

"I've been sleeping in the day and staying up every
night."

"True. But we've got to get you back on a better

schedule." David heard the seriousness, and he dreaded it. "David, I think you know it wouldn't work for you to stay here very long."

"I know."

"I won't bug you about anything tonight. But we've got to have a very good talk about your future. Okay?"

"Okay."

"I know there must have been a good reason or you wouldn't have run away. You don't have to tell me anything you don't want to tell me, but we have to figure out what you're going to do next."

David knew he didn't have long until she would press the issue, the way everyone else did, but he didn't let himself worry about that for now. He'd take the time he could have with her.

They finished their drinks, and then Melissa found some blankets and made a makeshift bed on the living room couch. "Okay," she said, "I'll leave so you can get undressed. The bathroom is right over there. I usually sleep pretty late. You better do the same in the morning. But if you wake up and want to turn the TV on or something, that's okay."

David nodded. He sat down and pulled off one of his shoes, not bothering to untie the knot.

"We'll go to the zoo tomorrow. And we need to think about getting you a few things. You don't even have a toothbrush, do you?"

"No."

"Well, we'll have to get you one." And then she knelt down by him. "Are you okay?"

"Sure."

"You laugh, but you always seem so sad."

"I'm not. I'm fine."

For several seconds she looked into his eyes, and David looked back, trying not to look sad, trying to say thank-you with his own eyes. Then she reached out and pulled his head over, held it against her cheek, ran her hand over his hair. "Oh, David, I'm sorry," she said.

"For what?" David held stiff, not sure that he could stand this.

"I don't know. Just sorry that life hasn't given you a better deal." David heard her voice shake. He couldn't take it. He pulled away from her. She looked at him then, nodded, and smiled, as if to say, "Everything's going to be all right." But David saw the tears in her eyes.

"I'll be okay," he said, and he gritted his teeth.

"We'll make things okay, little brother. We'll find a way." But a tear was rolling into the hollow of her lovely cheek.

David half believed she *could* do something. But when she was gone, he lay on the couch alone and realized that now he only had another problem, not an answer. He tried to get angry, but it just wasn't in him tonight.

12

David slept longer than he thought he might. When he woke, he could hear Melissa in the kitchen, and he could smell bacon. He reached down and grabbed his jeans, pulled them on while he was still covered, and then sat up and slid on the same shirt that he had worn the night before.

"David, you don't need to get up yet," Melissa called to him. "If you're tired, sleep some more."

David walked to the kitchen in his bare feet. "That's okay," he said. "I'm not tired."

"Well, you were sure sleeping like a log. I walked down to the corner and bought some groceries. We're going to have a real breakfast—bacon, eggs, and toast. How do you like your eggs?"

David shrugged.

"What does that mean? You don't like them, or you don't know which way?"

"I guess I like 'em scrambled best."

"Yeah, me, too. Besides, that's the easiest way to cook them. I'm not really much of a cook."

And so Melissa got breakfast ready, and the two of them talked. David liked passing the time with Melissa now that he was relaxing with her a little more. She kept the conversation going most of the time, but she didn't probe. Maybe for that reason David told her more about himself than he expected to. After breakfast they drove to a little shopping area and Melissa bought David some things he needed: a toothbrush and hairbrush, some socks and underwear, and another shirt—even though he had the shirts Elaine had bought him. She spent over forty dollars, and David was embarrassed about that. Melissa said not to worry; she liked doing it.

They went back to the apartment, just long enough for David to shower and change and brush his teeth, and then they drove to the zoo. It was a cool day, overcast, and not many people were there, but that was all the better. David and Melissa just strolled, took their time, and looked at what they pleased. Melissa kept talking to the animals, greeting them, asking how their day was going. David said she didn't speak their language, so she started trying. They laughed when she couldn't think of a sound to make to greet the giraffes.

They bought hot dogs for lunch and carried them along. Melissa fed most of hers to the animals. Eventually the sun came out, and the day was pretty, but a breeze was blowing, and it was still cold.

At one of the outdoor animal pits a lion was pacing back

and forth, rubbing its neck against the edge of a rock sometimes, but mostly covering the same path over and over. "I think he's lonely," Melissa said.

"It's a she."

"Oh, yeah. I guess that's right. Don't you think she's lonely? They have her in there all by herself."

"I think there are some more, but they're staying inside."

"Yeah. I guess."

Melissa kept watching. David watched her when he could. She had worn a heavier coat today, a red-and-blue parka. David could see the vapor escape from her mouth when she spoke, could see the gentleness in her eyes as she followed the lion's movements.

"I'm lonely a lot, David. I'm about like that poor lion. A lot of days I don't know what to do with myself. I get up at ten or so, and I have all those hours until I have to go to the hotel. When the weather's nice, I get out a lot. I go sit on the beach out by Shilshole Bay, or over on Lake Washington. Sometimes I drive up to the mountains. But lots of times that only makes me lonelier."

David took a chance. "I get lonely a lot, too."

She looked down at him. "But running away only makes that worse, doesn't it?"

"No."

"No? Why not?"

"It's just the same."

"Do you want to tell me why, or is that one of those things we don't get to talk about?"

David let his breath out, saw the steam drift away.

"Where I lived, I was really alone—in a way."

"Was it some kind of home, or was it with a foster family?"

"Foster family."

"And you didn't like them?"

David didn't know how to answer that one.

"Kiddo, you're something. I can tell when I've gone a little too far. I see that look come into your eyes, and it's like you just slide inside yourself and disappear."

David didn't like that at all. He didn't want her to feel that. "I don't. I mean . . . I just don't know what to say sometimes."

"That's okay." She ran the back of her hand along his cheek. "I really like you, David. You bring out something really good in me."

David was embarrassed, but he wanted to talk to her, to think of something he could say. "I think you're very nice," he said. He wanted to say more; he wanted to tell her how much he liked her. But the moment passed, and he didn't do it.

Melissa turned toward David, put her hand on his head. "Thank you," she said, but she looked sad. And then she added, "Aren't you cold? Don't you need your hood up?" She put her hands on his ears to check them.

"It's your hands that are cold, not my ears."

"I know. I'm cold. Do you care if we leave now?"

"No. We saw almost everything anyway."

"Gee, I'm doing what your dad used to do—making you leave too soon."

"No. That's okay."

118

They started to walk. "Why don't you marry Paul?" David asked. "He's nice."

"Paul?" she said, laughing. "Don't you think he's a little old for me?"

"I don't know. You said you wouldn't mind marrying him." She was walking with her hands tucked into her coat pockets. She leaned her head back and shook her long hair out, so it fell down over her coat. She was smiling, and then she started to laugh. "Oh, David. We would be some combination. Paul's a lonelier soul than I am."

"That's why you should be together."

She didn't take the idea seriously. David could see that. And in a moment, the quietness had returned to her eyes.

"David, do you go to church?" she asked.

"Sometimes."

"Were your parents religious? Did they go to church?"

"No. But the people I lived with—the last ones—went most of the time, and they took me."

"Did you like it?"

"I don't know. Not much."

"That's how I was. I guess that's how most kids are. I went. But I didn't really listen; I didn't even think about all that stuff. Now I don't know what I believe, or what life's supposed to mean. It just seems like there ought to be something more to it than what I've got now."

"Like what?"

"I don't know. I guess I need something—or some-one—to care about. I don't have anything like that now."

"I don't either."

"I know. And we can't let that happen to you. That's why everyone keeps telling you to go down and talk to Arnie."

It always came around to that. David didn't want another speech on that subject.

They had arrived at the car. Melissa had her keys out, but she didn't open the car yet. She looked down at David. "You're a little stranger, David. You look so lonely, and you speak so softly. I guess all of us at the hotel just want to take care of you. But there's not one of us who can take you in. So we look around for some other answer."

David thought he understood that. But he also knew they didn't really understand everything.

Melissa unlocked the door and let David in. But she didn't drive home. She drove out along Shilshole Bay. When David saw the wharves where the sailboats were docked, he thought he remembered seeing the place before. He vaguely remembered walking along the wharf, holding his mother's hand. But in his memory, the place was all blue and bright and warm, and Billy was there, laughing and talking a mile a minute.

By the time they got back to the apartment, it was late afternoon. Melissa made some soup, and she heated up a frozen pie she had bought that morning. "That's just so I can tell Rob that I furnish pie for you, too."

But eventually she had to leave for work. David put in a long evening. Melissa didn't have cable, and David didn't like most of the TV shows. He liked long movies, ones that grabbed his interest and held it.

He decided not to sleep, to wait up for Melissa. But the late movies were stupid, and he fell asleep in spite of his efforts. He woke up only when she had come in and was trying to pull off his shoe.

"Hi," he said.

"You go back to sleep. I was just going to pull some covers over you."

"Can we have some hot chocolate?" He sat up.

Melissa laughed softly. "I think not. You're still half-asleep."

"No, I'm not." He opened his eyes as wide as he could.

"Okay. I was going to have some anyway." She walked into the kitchen and got out the milk. David followed. "David, something has happened. I might as well tell you."

Something in her voice scared him.

"Ralph got talking to Howard today. Ralph asked him if Paul had really gotten rid of you. Howard said he didn't know anything about it—except that a kid was in the bellmen's room at the end of his shift last night."

David took a deep breath and held it. He could see what was coming.

"I wasn't there at the time, of course, but from what everyone is saying, Ralph really hit the ceiling. He was telling everyone that he's going to fire Paul. It was Paul's night off, so Ralph hasn't seen him yet. If it goes the way it usually does, Ralph will cool off and not do anything. He's been threatening to fire Paul for months."

"I'll bet he does this time."

"Well, maybe. I don't know. But Paul has been getting by all right for a long time. He has connections in hotels just about everywhere. He can find another job."

"But he came here so he wouldn't drink. If he goes back

to San Francisco, or somewhere like that, he'll start drinking again."

"I don't know, David. I wouldn't say that—not necessarily." She was leaning against the kitchen cabinet, her arms folded in front of her. "Maybe he will. I know what you're thinking. But it's not your fault. Ralph is going to get rid of him sooner or later. Or Paul will just leave. He never stays in one place too long."

But David couldn't accept that. "Melissa, he wants to stay at the Jefferson. He needs some friends. I don't think he wants to move around all the time anymore. I knew I was going to get him in trouble. I was going to leave every day, and then I didn't." David was standing in the kitchen doorway. He still had one shoe on.

Melissa slid her fingers into the front pockets of her jeans. "Why didn't you leave, David?"

"I don't know."

"It's interesting to me what you know and don't know. You see plenty. You understand a whole lot more than most kids your age. All this stuff about Paul, for instance. But as soon as I ask you why you do something, suddenly you tell me you don't know. I think you do." She was teasing a little, smiling, but David knew she was serious, too.

"I wanted to stay warm, and watch TV."

"Yeah, right. And that's the only thing?"

David looked at the floor. "I liked Paul. And Rob and Elaine."

"Hey! Anyone else?"

"Yeah. Clark and Betty."

She laughed, and then she waited until he looked at her.

"You know what you did a few minutes ago?"

"What?"

"You called me by my name. That's the first time you've done that."

David had known that. He had seen her react at the time. But now he hated knowing that he was blushing.

"David, what are you going to do?"

David shrugged. "I wanted to stay with Paul, but he can't take me." He was amazed at himself that he was admitting this, that he was talking so openly with Melissa now.

"That wouldn't work, David. You know that."

"Yeah, maybe it wouldn't."

"So what's plan two?"

David took a long breath, waited, took another, and then he said it. "Couldn't I stay here?"

When he finally looked up at her again, she was shaking her head slowly, smiling. "Oh, David, I'm a cocktail waitress, working night shifts. I'm twenty-three. I'm single. None of that works. You need a mom and a dad. You need to eat right. You need a nice house. You need to go to school and church, and Boy Scouts, and Little League and all that. I'm no one to give you that stuff."

David nodded and tried to look accepting. Above all, he didn't want to make her feel bad but he didn't believe any of it. He didn't care about houses or Boy Scouts—or any of the rest. He had taken a chance, actually asked, and he felt stupid now for doing it. Nothing was ever going to change. Why couldn't he learn not to start hoping? It was the same mistake he made every time.

13

David woke up the next morning thinking about Paul. He wondered if he couldn't go to the hotel and talk to Ralph. Maybe he could explain, show how everything was really his own fault, not Paul's. But Melissa didn't agree. She said that Ralph wouldn't listen to him. She would talk to Ralph herself if she got a chance, but she doubted it would make any difference.

Later in the afternoon, Melissa took David for a ride. She took the remains of a dried-up loaf of bread with her and stopped along the shores of Lake Washington, where she and David got out and fed the ducks. It was a pretty day, cool but bright, and the sky dark blue. Melissa talked to the ducks as though they were old friends. She told David they spoke English, that they had picked it up from her.

When Melissa went to work that night, David sat back

and watched TV. But he kept thinking about the day. He thought about how much he had laughed, and he kept seeing Melissa's face. When she had left that night, she had given him a hug. He remembered now how she smelled, how her face felt, touching his. He was embarrassed to think how he had begun to feel about her. If she knew, she would laugh at him. And David knew it was stupid, too, but he wished it weren't.

David waited up. He wanted to know about Paul, and he could tell that something was wrong as soon as she came in. Melissa made the hot chocolate, but she seemed preoccupied by something.

"Melissa," David finally said, "Paul got fired, didn't he?" He was sitting at the kitchen table. Melissa was mixing chocolate with the heated milk.

"Well, yes. Probably. Ralph gave him a week's notice. But he might not stick to it."

"What will Paul do?"

"I talked to him about that. He just laughed. He said he doesn't care."

"I still want to talk to Ralph."

"No, David. He wouldn't listen to you. But I'll tell you what it's time for. You're going to have to listen to me." She brought the mugs to the table and sat down across from David.

David made a very big slurp with his first spoonful, and she smiled a little, but he could tell she was serious. "Okay, I'm listening."

"David, I talked to Paul about you. We think the longer you stay around all of us, the worse things will get for you.

We like you, and that makes you comfortable, but it doesn't solve the problem. You've got to get back with a family." She took a sip from her spoon, didn't slurp at all. "I think you got put with the wrong family in the past. Someone made you feel unwanted, or something like that. So now you've got your mind made up it will always be like that. But it doesn't have to be. You've got to try again." She didn't know, didn't understand. And David knew he couldn't tell her. She was going to say he had to leave. He felt the blackness returning, the cold inside himself.

"Come on. Don't look like that. All you have to do is go talk to Arnie, and I'll go with you."

David knew what he had to do. He would leave in the morning.

"So here's what we're thinking. Arnie has some meeting he has to go to tomorrow, so it's not a good day for him. The next day is. Tomorrow we'll do something fun. And then tomorrow night Paul said to bring you down to the hotel. He wants to say good-bye to you, and so does everyone else. Then the next day we'll find you a family."

David was glad for the day—glad he didn't have to leave in the morning. He tried to concentrate on that. He had one nice day ahead, and he would see Paul and Rob and Elaine. The next morning he would leave. He would figure out how to get to California. Paul said that wouldn't work, but it was better than anything Paul could think of.

"David, will you do that?"

David couldn't look at her. He was sipping on his hot chocolate.

126

"Don't look so sad. You can probably come and visit us sometimes. In a few weeks you'll be happier than you've been in a long, long time. I really believe that. Will you do it?"

"Okay," David said, but he was lying to her. It was better that way.

Melissa smiled and reached over and touched his shoulder. "David, I'm glad you've been here with me awhile. I'm going to miss you."

David fought not to feel anything. He should have stayed one night in the hotel and then moved on. Sticking around had been the biggest mistake of all.

The next day David and Melissa drove up into the mountains. They stopped and looked at Snoqualmie Falls. They talked, and they laughed, but David found himself unable to enter into things the way they had the day before. Melissa seemed to know that or to feel much the same way. She was quieter. But she touched him more often, treated him like her little brother.

That evening, when she took David to the hotel, she told him to wait outside for a second, until she checked who was inside. But in a minute Paul came out. "Hey, partner," he said, "come on in." He reached toward David as though he weren't quite sure what to do. He ended up putting his hand on his shoulder and giving it a little shake.

"Won't you get in trouble?"

"Nah. What do I care anyway? A few more days and I'm out of here."

"I'm sorry I got you fired."

"No way. I wouldn't have lasted much longer. I have to get going after a while."

But it wasn't true. David heard that in his voice.

"Listen, the only one who isn't going to like having you around here is Howard. So you better come to the bell-men's room until he leaves and I get off. I don't really care if he sees you. He can tell Ralph whatever he wants to. But it's probably better for you not to hang around the lobby until the night shift comes on. I'll stick around for a while after shift. Maybe we can buy some of that pie you all like to eat at night, and we'll have us a little party."

"Okay."

"Melissa says you're going with her to Social Services tomorrow. Right?"

"Yeah."

"Great. I feel good about that. But you'll keep in touch, right?"

"I don't know where you'll be."

"Well, I'll get in touch with you and let you know where I end up." David heard the smoothness, the con, and he felt the pain pass between them, as they both agreed to accept the lie. Paul turned then, and the two went inside and into the bellmen's room. Paul had to leave soon after, and he was busy, but he came in when he could. There was a tenseness between them now, however, and Paul seemed to be working to think of things to say.

When Howard finally left, David walked out to the front desk. Rob took a look at him curiously, as though he didn't recognize him. "May I help you? Do you have your wife and children with you, sir, or will that be a single tonight?"

"The storage room is okay," David said, "if you'll put a TV in there."

"David, is that you?" Elaine looked out from around the switchboard. "Honey, just a minute."

David went behind the desk. Elaine spoke to someone, pushed a button, and then she pulled her headset off and came to David.

"I've got to hug my boy," she said, and she leaned over and pulled him close. "I've missed you, do you know that?"

David didn't answer. But he smiled at Elaine when she stepped back. "Who's been buying you more clothes?" she asked. "Did Melissa buy you that shirt?"

"Yeah."

"She's trying to steal you away from me. That's what she's trying to do."

"Come on, lady," Rob said. "Quit slobbering over the poor kid. We need to get down to some serious celebrating here. What can we do to give old Dave a big send-off?"

Paul was walking toward the desk now. "Let's buy some of this famous pie I keep hearing about," he said.

"Pie at eleven o'clock? I don't think we can do that. My digestive system doesn't expect pie until at least two-thirty."

"Quit your complaining, Rob." Everyone turned to see Betty, who had just come around the corner. "I'll even pay for it."

"Betty, what are you doing down here so late?"

"I came down to say good-bye to David. Paul told me this would be my last chance."

"That's nice, Betty," Elaine said. "But don't say it like that. David's going to come to visit us sometime—and tell us all about his new family."

"That's right," Paul said. "We'll all get together again." Everyone knew that wasn't true, what with Paul leaving, but no one said so. "So what kind of pie does everyone want? I'll go get it."

Rob decided he could maybe handle some now, and all the others put in their orders. Betty ended up going with Paul to make sure he could carry it. While they were gone Clark came to the desk. He asked David how he was doing. "I hear you're going to get set up with a family again. I'm glad to hear that. That'll be a lot better for you."

David nodded. Elaine said she was relieved David was willing to do that now. And Rob said, "That's right, my man. That's the best thing." And still David was nodding, a little sick inside, knowing what he was going to do in the morning.

When Paul and Betty got back with two sacks full of Styrofoam containers, Clark went for coffee. A man, arriving late, came to the desk, and Rob checked him in. But before long everyone was around the front desk, all eating pie, all laughing. Melissa came up the hallway and stuck her head out, and then came out to say hello to everyone.

"Aren't we something?" Elaine said. "If Mr. Raymond walked in here right now, he'd fire every one of us."

"Big loss," Rob said. "We'd all be better off."

"I don't think so," Elaine said. "I like this old place. And I like all of you. If it weren't for you people, I wouldn't have anybody."

Melissa said Elaine was right—that she felt the same way—and Betty agreed. The men looked at their pie. David watched Paul. He had stopped eating, but he didn't look at anyone. David wondered what he was thinking.

"Well, I've liked it here," Paul said, trying to sound offhanded. "This is a nice little house to work."

But David heard more. Paul wouldn't have these people now—or anyone else; he was leaving again.

Rob made a joke, and they all laughed, seemingly relieved to break the seriousness, and Melissa turned to go back to the bar.

"Wait a minute," Elaine said. "I brought my camera down. I want to get a picture of everybody together."

"Just a minute," Melissa said. "I've got to check what's happening in the lounge."

Elaine had everyone gather in front of the desk, David in the middle. At first she said that she didn't need to be in the picture, that she was too old and ugly anyway. But everyone insisted she be included. By then Melissa had come back.

"Get Cash to come up and take the picture," Paul said.

"Okay," Melissa said, "but we gotta all be ready first. And you're all standing wrong. This has to be a family pose. Paul and Betty, you're the mom and dad; you stand behind David. Clark and Elaine are the grandma and grandpa. You two get together, too."

Everyone was laughing, but Betty and Paul locked arms

and smiled at each other. Clark moved over by Elaine, and she grabbed his arm and planted a big kiss on his cheek. He chuckled a little and muttered something about not having been kissed for a long time. The two couples formed the back row, and Melissa moved David to the center. "Okay," she said, "Rob and I will kneel down next to David. We're the big sister and big brother." And then she was off to get Cash, the bartender, to take the picture.

Cash came up, grinning, looking at the strange collection. "Hey, you really do look like a family," he said. "You're about as weird looking as mine."

Melissa hurried over and kneeled next to David, putting her arm around his shoulder. "I'm the tramp of a sister who ran off to be a bar girl," she said.

"We're all glad you came back," Rob said. "Give your brother a great big kiss."

"All right," she said, and she leaned over and kissed David on the cheek.

"No, no. Your other brother."

"I could go for this," Betty was saying at the same time. "I've had the hots for Paul for a long time."

"Hey, come on," Cash said. "Quit talking and give me a big smile." The flash went off and a buzz followed, and the film pushed its way out of the bottom of the camera. Cash wanted to get back to the bar but Elaine wouldn't let him. She made him take seven pictures, one for each person "in the family."

David stood in the middle, everyone close around him, joking and telling him what a great kid they had. Elaine gave the last picture to David. He stood with it, watching as it came into focus. He laughed when he saw Rob grinning and Betty gripping Paul so tight. What he couldn't stand to do was look at the real people, who were all still hovering about him.

14

David woke up early the next morning—at least early considering how late he had gone to bed. He guessed it was around eight. He had to leave now. He had promised himself when he had gone to bed that he wouldn't consider any other possibility. He would just get up and go.

Now, however, as he slid his jeans on, he wondered what Melissa would think. He didn't want her to worry about him. Before he put his shoes on, he tiptoed to the kitchen. He knew there was a pen and a pad of paper by the phone. He picked up the pen and stared at the paper, trying to think what to say. The only thing he wanted to tell her was, "I love you," but he couldn't say that. It was stupid.

Finally he wrote, "I had to go. I'm sorry. David." He set the note on the little kitchen table.

He went back and put his coat on. He looked at the clothes Elaine had given him, and the ones from Melissa. He pulled another shirt on, over the one he had put on first, and stuffed a pair of socks in each pocket. He checked to make sure he had his pocketknife. He didn't want to carry anything else. He hoped Elaine and Melissa wouldn't be offended.

He went to the door, opened it quietly, and went out. But it was then, shutting the door, that he lost his nerve. The thought of never seeing her again suddenly brought back all the feelings he had been fighting for two years. He held the door, almost shut, and thought of walking back in, at least going to her door and looking at her one more time. But she might wake up. Besides, he told himself, she didn't want him to stay any longer. If he stayed she would only take him to Social Services and get rid of him.

David shut the door, and he decided to be angry. She and Paul were the same. The only thing Paul had ever tried to do was get rid of him. David walked down the stairs and out the front door. The morning was cold. He pulled the hood of his coat up and headed down the hill. He was not really sure where he was going.

A couple of blocks down the street David came to a little convenience store and gas station. He was wondering about maps. Sometimes gas stations gave away maps.

Inside, however, David saw doughnuts in a glass case on the counter. He was surprised to realize he was hungry, but he also knew he would get a lot hungrier. He decided not to spend any of his money yet. He only had eight dollars. He didn't know how long it would have to last.

"Hello," the young man at the counter said. "What do you need?"

"Do you have any maps?"

"Yeah, a few. What did you want? Washington or—"

"California."

"Yeah. We have that." The boy came out from behind the counter and walked to a magazine shelf. He looked for a minute and then pulled a California map from a little wire rack.

"Does it cost anything?"

"Afraid so. Buck and a half."

David knew he couldn't spend that much of his money on a map. He was embarrassed. "I guess I won't get it," he said.

"Okay. Whatever." The guy stuck the map back.

"Do you know how to get to California from here?"

"Yeah. Sure. Straight down the freeway—south on I-5."

"Thanks." David walked to the door and pulled his hood back on. "Can you tell me where the freeway is from here?"

The boy looked confused, maybe suspicious. "Sure. But who's doing the driving?"

"My dad. My parents are going on a trip. They asked me to find out for them."

"They don't know how to get to the freeway?"

"We're not from here." David knew the kid didn't believe him. He decided he better just get out. He pushed on the door.

"Hey, wait a sec. The freeway is down off the hill, but you have to go over about six blocks to hit an on-ramp."

"Thanks," David said, and he went out. He walked quickly. At the edge of the parking lot he glanced back, and he saw the boy at the door, watching. He hoped the kid didn't suspect what was going on, wouldn't call the police.

David headed down the hill. He wondered how soon Melissa would wake up. What would she think of him? What would she do? He wasn't doing very well at staying angry, but he told himself he had to get out of Seattle. He had to get away from the cold, and away from . . . everyone.

He walked a long way before he came to a place where he could see the freeway. The guy had pointed to the left; about six blocks he had said, to where an on-ramp was. So David walked that way. The morning was gray, the fog hanging over the tall downtown buildings across the freeway. It wasn't raining, but a mist was in the air. He felt the cold and wet sinking into him, even though he was walking fast.

He had thought of hitchhiking to California since the day he had left the Poulters' house—but he knew the risks. Someone might pick him up and take him right to the police; or worse, someone might try to hurt him. What he really needed was more money, enough to buy a bus ticket. But he had no idea where he could get that, and so he had to take his chances on the freeway.

What he found at the freeway entrance, however, was a sign that said "No Hitchhiking." He watched the traffic, moving very fast even on the on-ramp. He wasn't sure anyone could—let alone, would—stop for him.

For a couple of minutes David waited on the corner. He

didn't know how far California was, but he knew it was a long way. Even if he got a ride, how could he keep getting rides? But what else could he do?

David walked up the on-ramp to the freeway. Cars were coming by very fast, the wind from them whipping against his coat, even making it hard for him to keep his balance. He stuck out his arm, extended his thumb, felt the cold on his bare hand. He saw the glances, as drivers shot by, but no one seemed to give a second thought to stopping.

The blur of cars in the busy morning traffic was almost constant, and it didn't take long for David to see a hopelessness in the steady stream. But each time he thought of walking back down the ramp, what faced him was the blackness of no purpose at all.

And then a car slowed, rather suddenly. David saw the blur of black and white and realized it was a police car. At the same moment, he was running, down the on-ramp and onto the street, and then down the hill. He glanced up only once, saw nothing. The policeman had no hope of getting back to David in all the traffic. But he might radio someone else. David had seen that sort of thing in movies. And so he dodged through a back alley to another street and kept hurrying down into the busier part of the city.

Once he saw no sign that anyone was chasing him, he realized he had no place to go. He tried to think what he could do. What he needed was a job of some kind, but he had no idea how to find one.

He kept moving, as much as anything to stay warm. He tried to think of his options, but what he felt was a loneliness beyond anything he had known before. The night he left the Poulters' house, he had felt some sense of relief, of escape, but now he only felt loss. He had also known, then, that he would get to California somehow; he hadn't faced the reality of actually trying to get there. A sort of panic began to build inside. He knew he had to think of something, some plan, something to put some hope in.

He realized then that he was actually making his way toward the old Pike Street farmers' market downtown. When he had stalled away some time there before, he had thought that maybe one of the produce salesmen would give him a job. If nothing else, he could get down to the lower floors, inside the building where the old shops were, and he could stay out of the wind.

By the time he reached the market, he was telling himself he would ask at every vegetable stand, every fish market, until someone gave him some work. If he could save a few dollars a day, he suspected he would have enough for a bus ticket before long.

He began to feel a little better as he concentrated on his plan. He walked the last few blocks resolutely. The morning traffic was busy, and lots of people were on the streets, which was all sort of encouraging, but he was passing through a pretty tough part of town, full of pawn shops and neglected old buildings. He could smell Elliott Bay— the stink of the ocean in the moist grayness of the morning fog. And then he passed a wino on the street, a filthy man with tangled hair and beard, and an old wool coat with most of the buttons gone. Something in the man's face— the blankness—unnerved David. He felt himself shaking all over.

But he kept walking. He tried not to think about anything but the job he would find. What came to mind, however, was the hotel room, the clean smell of lemon and the feel of the ironed sheets. He longed for that warmth, that cleanliness. And he thought of Melissa's kitchen, with the bright flowered wallpaper, thought of the way she had talked to him in that gentle voice.

As David turned down the street that looped through the market area, he saw the stands, saw the men setting up for the day. He lost his courage in the same instant. He wasn't sure he could approach them. What would he say? What kind of questions would they start asking? As he got closer, he saw how busy people were. They wouldn't want to be bothered now.

He would wait. He would spend a little money and get something to eat. And then he would begin asking. It was a new plan. It was a purpose. He would wait an hour or so, and then he would look for work.

David found a little coffee shop, inside the market, and he sat down at a counter and ordered a doughnut and a cup of hot chocolate. And then he took as much time eating as he could. He let the chocolate cool, didn't slurp it, but the taste brought back thoughts he didn't want.

"Don't you need to get to school?"

The guy behind the counter had not paid much attention to David at first, but the little place was clearing out now. He walked down to David, stood in front of him. He was a big, dark man with a bulging stomach and a stained white apron. He had shaved carelessly, leaving patches of stubble on his chin.

"Uh . . . no," David said. He tried to think what he could say.

"What'ya doing? Playing hookey?" He had some sort of accent.

"No." David took the last bite of his doughnut. He would have to leave now.

"So what's today? A holiday?"

"Yeah. The teachers have a meeting."

The man nodded, seemed to accept the explanation. "You like that, huh?"

"Yeah."

"So what'cha doing down here?"

David didn't know what to say for a moment. "Looking for a job," he finally said.

"Where? Upstairs in the market?"

David nodded.

"Nah. You're too little. They only need big boys up there. Most of the guys got kids anyway. They don't hire nobody else."

David didn't need this. "I want to make some money," he said, almost to himself.

"What you need money for? Don't your old man give you none?"

David didn't answer. But he felt some trust in this big, friendly man. He decided to ask. "I need to get to California. I need bus money."

"How come California?"

"I just need to go there. I was going to hitchhike, but cars won't stop on the freeway."

"No, no, no. Don't do that. Someone gonna hurt you, you do that."

"How can I get there then?"

"You running away?"

"No." David tried to think of something. "My big brother's down there. He's married. I'm going to live with him."

"Don't he got no money he can send you?"

"No."

Now the man looked skeptical. He picked up David's empty plate and cup, whisked a wet rag across the counter. "Maybe some of these truck drivers up on the street might give you a ride. But they gonna say the same thing. They gonna think you running away."

It was an idea. David paid for his food, and he went upstairs. He hesitated for some time before he approached a truck driver, but he finally got up the nerve to ask. The man told him, however, that he just delivered locally, that not many of the men who stopped at the market traveled out of state. He said that if David wanted a ride to California, he would have to ask at the big truck stops south of town, near the freeway. He also said that most guys wouldn't take on riders. But David had a new purpose. He got more instruction where one of the trucks stops was, and he began to walk. He was even glad to know he had a very long way to go. That would take some hours, give him a plan that would last awhile.

David was tired when he reached the truck stop that the man had told him about. He had gotten mixed up and walked well out of his way, and he had covered quite a few miles. The day had warmed some, and David had tried not to think about the hotel or Paul or Melissa. He had been all right. But as he approached the little restaurant at the truck stop, he knew he had to ask people again, and that was frightening.

It was afternoon now. David was hungry. Inside, he smelled the food. He decided to spend some money for a hamburger. He had to eat one good meal, he told himself. And so he sat in a booth and ate, and he put off approaching anyone yet. He heard the talk of the people in the restaurant, mostly men, and all the laughter and the loud talk. He tried to spot someone he wouldn't be afraid to ask.

But he let most of the people go, and he sat in the booth sipping his Coke long after he had finished eating. He eventually heard the word "California." He turned and looked at a man who was sitting on a stool at the counter. He was fairly young, was wearing a baseball cap, and he was laughing, making jokes with the waitress. David waited a little longer, but finally he got up the nerve to walk over to the counter and slide up on the stool next to the man.

The man looked at David and grinned. He grabbed the bill of his baseball cap, tipped it just a little. "Hey, partner, how're you doing?"

"Okay."

The man looked back toward the waitress, but David said, "Are you going to California?"

"Sure am."

"Do you think maybe I could ride with you?"

The man turned now, looked David straight on. "What do you want to do in California?"

"I have a brother down there. I'm going to live with him."

"Whereabouts?"

David was stunned. He hadn't thought about this. He tried to think of the name of any cities. "San Francisco," he finally said, but he knew the man had seen his confusion.

"Well, that's not where I'm going. I'm heading into Sacramento, and then west from there."

"If I could get to California, I could probably get another ride to San Francisco."

The man took a long look at David. "How old are you?" he asked.

"Twelve."

"What do your folks have to say about all this?"

"They say it's okay."

"They say it's okay for you to hitch rides all the way to California?"

"Yeah."

"What's your name?"

David hesitated just an instant, and then he said, "David."

"Okay, David, how about if I call your folks and see if it's all right?"

"They're not home right now. They both work."

The man laughed, rather loudly, and he glanced over at the waitress. She was smiling. "Son, do I look dumb? Is that why you picked me out?"

"I heard you say you were going to California." But David had given up. He started to slide off the stool.

"First of all, I think you're running away from home, or something like that. Second, I ain't about to turn a little kid like you loose on the street somewhere and say, 'Good luck, hope you get another ride.' Third, I could get thrown in the clink for transporting a runaway kid across state lines. Fourth, my company don't allow us to pick up no hitchhikers. And fifth, and this is the big one—you need to head on home right this minute."

David took a step away from the man, headed for the door. But then he heard him say, "Son, it ain't gonna work. No trucker's going to take that kind of chance."

David kept going. He left the truck stop and started back the way he had come—not because he was going anywhere, but because he didn't know what else to do. He was trying not to panic, not to let himself break down. He knew he would have to think of something else. He had walked a couple of blocks before he realized that he had never paid for his hamburger. He stopped for a moment, thought of going back, but couldn't bear to do that. All the same, he was ashamed of himself. It wasn't something he had meant to do.

15

David was sitting on a bench in Pioneer Square. On the other end of the bench was an old man, a bum, who was sleeping with his head on his chest, his long hair falling over his face. David had walked a very long way, and his feet were tired. He had no plan now. Somehow he had to earn some money. He was sure of that again, but he didn't know how.

As the sun began to go down, early, it crossed his mind that he would go back to the hotel or maybe try to call Melissa. But he couldn't do that. She or Paul might take him back in for a day or two, but then they would start to talk about going to Social Services again. However much he hated what was happening to him, he still believed there was something worse. This bench was not better, but California still was, if he could just find a way to get there. If he gave up believing that, nothing was left.

But the sun was going down fast, and a mist was in the

air. It wasn't rain, just a fine spray that floated more than fell and blew with the wind. He had pulled the drawstring on his hood so tight that very little of his face was exposed, and he held his arms close around himself, his hands deep in his coat pockets. All the same, he was shivering, and he knew he would have to start walking or get inside somewhere, but his feet ached so bad he hated to start out again.

David spent the evening in stores, as much as possible, sitting down where he could, and when outside he walked until he was hobbling on blisters and aching legs. He had sat inside storefronts at times, or in blind alleys, but always the cold had forced him back into the streets, walking.

The night passed slowly, but at least it was passing, or so he thought. And then he stopped in front of a store, a run-down little-used bookstore. He stared at the clock, trying to believe that it had stopped, that the time couldn't be right. But the second hand was turning steadily, slowly, and the other hands said it was only one-thirty. David had been certain it was four or five, that the sun would be coming up soon. When he felt tears on his face, he didn't bother to wipe them away.

Police were about, and David had avoided their cars, or the ones walking, by slipping into dark alleys. But now he wondered. Maybe he would let them pick him up. Maybe this all wasn't worth it. All evening some stubbornness had held in him, and he had tried to think only of getting through this night, nothing beyond. And that had worked until now. But the clock was too much. He knew no way that he could last that many more hours. He wasn't sleepy;

he wasn't even scared. He was just out of strength, and he was freezing from inside out.

He hadn't looked up the street for a time. He had been watching the clock too long. The voice he heard startled him, and he jerked around to see who was speaking. "Hey, boy, come here. I need some help."

David heard the slur of alcohol on the man's voice, saw the bulky layers of coats hunched over his shoulders. The guy was a wino, David was sure. In the dark, he saw no face, only the silhouette of a floppy hat, pulled over straggly hair.

"Come here, boy."

"No." David took a step back.

"I need some help. My friend fell down. He hurt his face."

David was edging back, unwilling to take his eyes off the man, but ready to make his break.

"I ain't gonna hurt you. My friend's hurt. I gotta carry him 'cross the street to that building right there. Thass a flophouse. I gotta get him in out of the cold or he's gonna freeze."

"No," David said, but he didn't run. He thought the man was telling the truth.

"He's right back there. He just tripped and fell down. I can't carry him by myself. What you doing out here anyway?" David didn't answer, and the man didn't seem to care. "Come on. Juss help me get him over there. You can sleep there, too. You need a place to go? It costs two dollars. Maybe Mel will let you sleep on the floor if you ain't got the two bucks."

David didn't know about that, but he wondered about

the man who was hurt. This drunk was not going to be able to help him. And so he walked up the street, keeping his distance from the man. He soon saw the dark lump on the street.

A faint light from a neon sign farther up the street was casting a yellow tint across the sidewalk. David came close to the man, however, before he saw the pool of blood. He stopped, thought of running, but stood rigid. The drunk who was walking behind David was huffing with every step, and he took some time catching up. David took a couple of steps away, but he watched as the man knelt by his friend and then rolled him over.

In the yellow light, the blood was purple, but worse than that was the caved-in face. The man's nose was gone, smashed into his face, and his forehead was flattened—as though he had been struck with an iron. David didn't want to see this, but he didn't look away.

The drunk man wailed at the sight. "Oh, no. Oh, no," he said. "He's killed himself. He's gone and killed himself."

David wanted to ask whether the man was sure. He thought they should find a police car or call an ambulance, but he couldn't move. He hadn't known a face could break like that—that the bones would give way so easily. How could a head be crushed, as though it were just some kind of thing—like a plaster statue?

"He's dead. All he did was just trip and fall, and now he's dead."

"We better get an ambulance."

"What for? He's dead. Can't you see that?" The man stood up. "I'm getting out of here. Ain't nobody gonna blame this on me. He just tripped and went down, flat on his face. Thass all that happened."

The man stood for a time, still mumbling under his breath and sometimes letting out that strange wailing sound. Then he tromped away into the darkness, huffing as he stepped. When he was a long way off, David still heard his steps on the quiet street, and then the wailing sound again, like a child crying.

David stood there alone, looked down at the face and the blood. He hadn't known. He hadn't seen his parents or Billy. When he had come back to consciousness he had been in the ambulance. He had only seen them later, in their caskets, dressed up. He had had no idea that their bodies were so frail.

David had to do something. He couldn't just keep standing there. He finally got himself going and then, suddenly, he was running. He headed across the street to the flophouse. There was a desk inside, but no one around. He had to ring the bell half a dozen times before a skinny little man came out from a door behind the desk. "Yeah, yeah," he said, but then he looked surprised to see David.

"Excuse me. A man is out there on the street. He fell and hurt himself. I think he's dead."

"Is he a wino?"

"I guess so."

The man nodded, as if to say he thought so. "Who are you?"

"I was outside and a man asked me to help him carry the guy over here. But then he said he was dead and he left."

"Yup. That's how these bums do things. But what are

you doing out on the street?" The man tried to smooth down his sparse hair. When David didn't answer, he said, "You on the run?"

David struggled. He didn't think he was—not exactly. "Are you going to do anything for that man?"

"Yeah, I'll call," he said, but when he saw David start toward the door, he added, "Where you going?"

"I don't know."

"It's cold out there, ain't it?"

"Yeah."

The man shook his head and swore. Then he jerked his thumb over his shoulder. "Go back in there. You can sleep on the floor."

David walked into the room. The man had been sleeping on a cot. The smell was bad, like dirty laundry. David sat on the floor and leaned against the wall. He didn't think he could sleep, but he would stay warm, and he would rest. When he shut his eyes, he saw the purple blood, the face, the flattened forehead. For a time he thought he was going to vomit, but then his body stopped shaking and soon after seemed to leap toward sleep.

David woke up early, curled up on the floor. A blanket had been thrown over him. The man was gone. David sat up and only then felt the agony in his body. His legs and feet ached, and so did his back and shoulders. His head was numb.

But when his eyes went shut, he saw the face again, the smashed face. He tried to think what he had thought when he looked at it. His family had gotten themselves broken, that was all. And then he thought of Mr. Poulter—what he had said. Maybe he was right. Maybe everything he had said about David was right.

He sat still, trying to concentrate through the numbness, trying to think whether it was true. People had liked him at the hotel. It had been different there. Why?

But he couldn't answer that. He didn't know what had happened to him in the hotel. What he did know was that he had to set some things right. He couldn't just run away again until he had done that.

David waited until seven o'clock, and then he set out walking. His feet ached with every step, but he kept going. It wasn't all that many blocks to the hotel, and he had a purpose now. When he reached the hotel, he stepped inside the glass doors but stayed back where no one at the front desk could see him. Ralph was not at the bellmen's desk.

It wasn't long before he got off an elevator, however, and came strolling into the lobby. David motioned to him. Ralph laughed a little, and then he walked over. "Kid, I didn't think I'd see you sticking your nose in this place again."

"I need to talk to you."

"Yeah, well, I need to call the police—the way Paul should've done the first time he seen you. He'd still have a job now, if he'd done that, and you'd be back with your folks the way you need to be."

"I came here to ask you not to fire Paul. It wasn't his fault."

Ralph laughed, the air sucking under his tight upper lip. He raised his hand to cover his mouth. "Look, kid, Paul put you in a room that wasn't paid for. Worse than that, he put the hotel in a bad position by harboring a kid who had run away from home. That's serious business. I was stupid enough to let him get away with it the first time, and all he done was take advantage of me. So that's that. He's fired. Now come over here and let's call the police. We'll get you taken care of."

But David knew what Ralph really wanted. He just wanted to scare David away, have him out of his hair.

"Couldn't you just give Paul another chance? He won't do something like that again."

"Oh, brother. Look, kid, you don't know nothing about nothing. It ain't your problem. Paul hates my guts. He goes out of his way to tell me I don't know nothing about hotels. Well, maybe he don't think I know anything, but I'm his boss, and he knows that now. He never could figure that out."

David knew he might as well give up, but he didn't. He wanted to make things right somehow, and he kept trying to think what else he could say.

"Look, Paul don't even care," Ralph said. "He told me what I could do with this job. He said he's glad to be out of here."

"But he's not. All his friends work here."

This was a great joke to Ralph. He burst into laughter and then clapped his hand over his mouth, hiding the decayed teeth. "Oh, kid, that's a rich one," he said. "Paul don't have no friends. Paul don't even like anybody around here. He's a loner, man. He comes in for work and leaves when his shift is over. That's it."

"That's because . . ." But David didn't know how to explain what he was thinking. "He just doesn't talk a lot, but he likes people."

"No, kid. That's what you don't get. Paul don't like nobody. Maybe he felt sorry for you, but in the long run, he don't want you to be no weight around his neck. He stays to himself. But he uses people. He knows how to talk real sweet when he wants something. But that's just his con. You can't trust the man."

It was the same thing Paul had said, but David still didn't believe it.

"Look—I'll tell you what. If Paul will come to me and tell me he's sorry, that he knows who the boss is around here, and admit that just maybe I know as much about the hotel business as he does—then I'd be happy to give him his job back. All he's gotta do is beg me a little. You tell him that. You see what he says to you. You'll find out how much he cares about this job. He'd rather starve to death than treat me like his boss."

"What if he just said—"

"Kid, I don't have time for this. I'm walking to the phone right now. I'm calling the cops. I recommend you stand right here and wait for 'em. That would be the best thing for you. I ain't gonna try to hang onto you. Some lawyer would probably try to slap me in jail for child abuse—that's how things are these days. But I'm calling and you decide if you're waiting for them to get here."

David didn't answer. He walked out through the glass doors. He didn't hurry. He turned and watched Ralph walk to the phone at the bellmen's desk, but he knew

Ralph was bluffing. David knew some things about cons himself.

What he didn't know was where he was going. He only knew where he wanted to go. He took another look at Ralph and then turned farther around when he saw Betty coming toward the front doors. She came out to him. "David, what are you doing? I thought you were with Melissa."

"I had to leave," David said, unable to think of anything else.

"What are you planning to do?"

"Where does Paul live?"

"Around the corner. It's a little hotel there on Pike Street. I'm not even sure what it's called. Are you going over there?"

"Yeah. How far down the block is it?"

"It's almost to the next corner. It's got an old striped canopy over the entrance."

"Okay. I guess I'll go over there."

"Is that what Paul wants?"

"I don't know. Probably not. But I guess I'll go over there anyway."

16

David found the hotel and went inside. An old
man at the desk called upstairs and then said, "Okay. You
can go on up. Room two-oh-six. Second floor. The stairs
are faster, right over there."

When David got to the second floor he saw Paul standing in his open doorway, no shoes or shirt on, his belt not
buckled. "Down here," he said.

David didn't expect Paul's room to be very nice, but he
was still surprised by the darkness, the stale smell. Faded,
yellowed wallpaper hung from one corner of the room,
and a window blind was torn almost in half. An old sink
in the corner was stained orange under the dripping
faucet.

"David, what's going on?" Paul said. "Why'd you take
off?"

David shrugged.

"Hey, come on. We made a deal. You were going to

go see Arnie yesterday." He motioned for David to sit down on an old overstuffed chair, and he sat on his unmade bed. David could tell he had gotten Paul out of bed. He looked really tired. The circles beneath his eyes were dark as bruises. "David, this is stupid. You know that, don't you?"

"I guess so."

Paul ran his fingers through his hair and leaned forward, his elbows on his knees. He was wearing an undershirt that looked sort of yellow and was torn under one arm. "Tell me why you took off, David."

"I didn't want to go to another family."

"But why are you so set against that?"

"I guess I'm not anymore. I guess I'll have to do it." David felt strange saying the words without feeling any emotion. The truth of the situation had already hardened into reality.

"But you still don't like the idea?"

"No."

"Why not?"

David stared at the worn-out carpet, wondered whether Paul could understand. "They didn't want me."

"The family you were with? They took you, and then they didn't want you?"

David nodded.

"Hey, well, that kind of thing can happen. That doesn't mean—"

"Not just once."

"What do you mean? What else happened?"

David knew he had to tell it all, from the beginning. That's the only way Paul would ever understand. "When my dad and mom got killed, and I was still in the hospital, a man came to see me. He said nobody wanted me."

"What?"

"He told me I had no place to go, because no one would take me."

"Didn't you have any relatives?"

"They couldn't find any of my dad's family. He hadn't kept in touch with anyone. My mom has two sisters. But one was divorced, and she has three kids, and her husband doesn't give her any money. That's what she said anyway. And the other one said her husband was out of work."

"You mean they both just said they wouldn't take you?"

David nodded.

"Don't you have any grandparents?"

"I have a grandpa—my mom's dad—in Arizona. He couldn't come up to the funeral. They called him and he said I would be better off with a foster family. He didn't think he could do a good job of raising me. He said he was sick."

Paul swore softly. "What a world," he said. "So where did they put you?"

"First I was in the hospital—for a few days—and then after the funeral they put me at this detention place with guys who had all been in trouble. That was just a few days, too. And then they put me with a family, but they said I wouldn't be there very long. They were going to find me someone I could stay with all the time."

But David wasn't telling it right. He didn't know how to say what he had felt. He had cried every night in those days, had thought of nothing but that he would never see his family again, and every day the woman would say,

"One of these days you'll be going to a nice family." And she kept her distance, like a kid who finds a stray dog but doesn't want to get too attached, in case the owner comes along.

"Didn't they ever find you a decent family?"

"I don't know." Again, David didn't know how to explain what it had been like. "They put me with some people up in Snohomish. They had some other foster kids. They got money for taking kids in."

"Were they mean to you or anything?"

"No." David thought of the cold house, the woman who tried to hug him but who did it stiffly. "I was there almost a whole year of school. But then they said they couldn't keep any kids anymore. They didn't tell me why. I was in that place with all the boys again for about a week, and then I got put with another family for a month or so. But they told me that was just for a while again. And then they moved me to another place. It was a man and wife without any kids. Their name was Poulter."

"Where? In Seattle?"

"Up in Everett." David remembered the quiet in the house. Mr. Poulter had tried to be a father, at least at first, but he didn't know how. Mrs. Poulter had worried constantly about her house. She warned David every time he moved. The two of them would sit in the family room, Mr. Poulter reading the newspaper or a book, Mrs. Poulter reading, too, or doing crossword puzzles. David had almost never spoken, and the hours sitting there had always seemed like punishment.

"What happened there?"

David described it all, as best he could.

Paul listened, nodding. "So how long were you there?"

"I stayed the rest of the summer and this fall, until now. But they didn't like me."

"Come on, David. What are you talking about? Why wouldn't they like you?"

"I didn't do very good in school. And they kept telling me I had to practice reading more. Mr. Poulter always told me I wasn't trying. I would read to him and he would get so mad he would yell at me."

"Did he hit you?"

"No. But he got so he hated me. He finally said that they had taken me on trial, but it wasn't working out. He said his wife had wanted a child all her life, and now she didn't even want to try again. He said that's what I had done to her."

Paul hung his head, ran his fingers through his hair; he swore again. After a time he looked up. "Okay, David. I see better now what you've been through. But not everybody's some uptight old . . . guy, like that. There are some real nice people out there who want a kid. Maybe some who couldn't have any of their own, or something like that."

"They want little babies," David said. "That's what the man told me. He said it was hard to find people who would take a kid my age." David had never forgotten that—the sense that he would always be somebody's burden, somebody's problem.

"He never should have said that to you."

"He might as well. It's true. That's what people want."

"Some of 'em. But not everyone. There's got to be

someone out there who would like to have an older kid—a nice kid."

David had to say it. "Mr. Poulter told me no one would ever like me."

"Oh, come on. I'll bet he didn't say that. He probably just—"

"He said I was 'cold as an iceberg.' He was screaming, and he said a whole bunch of stuff. He said I wouldn't talk, that I wouldn't be friends with him. He said he had tried to be my friend, but I wouldn't be friends back. He said I hated him for no reason at all—it wasn't his fault my parents got killed. Then he said, 'No one's ever going to like you. No one can. You're too full of hate.'"

Paul cursed, and then he sat up straight and pointed a finger at David. "Look, David, that's just pure . . . junk. He had no right to say that to you. You don't have an ounce of hate in you. Not a single ounce."

David looked down at the floor, but he told the truth. "Yeah, I do. I wasn't nice to him. I was mad all the time back then. When he talked to me, I just kept my mouth shut. Then he quit talking, too. But it was my fault."

"Why didn't you want to talk to him?"

"I don't know. For a long time I cried all the time. That's all I wanted to do. And then I just decided to be mad so I wouldn't cry. And every time I went to another place, I did it more."

"So who were you mad at?"

"I don't know. I was just mad because somebody took my family away."

"No one took them. They just had some lousy luck."

David thought of the drunken man falling on his face, saw the flattened forehead again. "I know," he said.

"So what did you do? Run away right after this Poulter guy said that to you?"

David remembered that night. He had gone to his room and thought things over, and he decided Mr. Poulter was right about no one liking him. Nobody liked him at school either. Nobody had wanted him, not at first, and not at any of the places he had been. And so he had promised himself: He would run away, go to California, make it on his own somehow. But he wouldn't go to another family and be hated again, no matter what happened. He had promised himself that. He had left with nothing but his clothes and a few dollars that were his. And Billy's pocketknife— the one thing he valued most.

"Is that when you took off?"

"Yeah."

"And now you're telling yourself the next family will be the same way?"

"I don't know."

"What then?"

"They might not be just the same. But after a while they won't like me. And then it will all happen again."

"Oh, David." Paul slid back across the bed, leaned against the wall, with his legs stretched out in front of him. He rubbed his eyes with his fingertips. "Look, I don't blame you for feeling that way. But look what happened at the hotel. Everyone liked you, didn't they? Maybe it will be like that."

David did wonder about that. He didn't know why people had chosen to like him.

"David, sooner or later you have to stay put and make the best of things—even if it isn't what you think you want."

"I know."

"I know what you would really like, but it just can't happen. I know you'd like to stay on with Melissa, but think about it. She's just a kid herself. She—"

"I know. She told me all that."

Paul sat for quite some time. David glanced up at him a couple of times, but he was leaning back, his eyes shut, his jaw tight. "David, you gotta know I can't take you. I'm getting out of this dump, but I don't know where I'm going. I won't even have a job for a little while. I'll get something, but I don't know where yet."

"I know."

"Do you? You say that, but I don't think you really understand. You don't really know what kind of guy I am. There's just no way I could do it."

"I know. You told me that before."

"Do you see what it comes down to, David? No matter what has happened to you before, you just gotta try again. It might go a lot better this time."

David nodded. He didn't know whether he believed it, but it was the only thing left.

"David, I think someone's going to like you the way everyone at the hotel did. That ought to give you some confidence. And if it isn't great, it's not forever. It'll go fast. A few years from now you'll be out of high school, and then you can do all right for yourself. You're a smart kid. You got your whole life ahead of you. I think your luck is going to start running different now."

David heard the tone he didn't like—the con. "What about you? What are you going to do?"

"Get out of here. Find another job. Try to save a little money."

"I talked to Ralph. He said you could stay at the Jefferson."

"What? When did you talk to him?"

"Just now. He said if you came to him and said you were sorry, he would let you come back."

Paul laughed. "You gotta be kidding. I'm supposed to apologize to that jerk?"

"Yeah. And just say you know he's the boss, and you'll treat him that way from now on."

David saw the flash. "That . . ." Paul held back the words, but David knew how angry he was. "He knows I won't do that. The creep. He just wanted you to tell me that, to make me mad."

"I know. But you could do it."

"Sure, I could. But what for? I don't need that job."

"You need your friends at the hotel."

Paul laughed. "Look, David, I've never worked more than a few years at a place in my whole life. Most people who work hotels are like that. I don't really have any friends. I've had some drinking buddies, but I guess I've never had someone I'd call a friend in my whole life."

"Is that how you always want it to be?"

Paul looked at David for a time before he said, "I don't know, David. I like the people at the hotel, but we're all different from each other. We're not as close as you think we are. We just kind of got together for a little while because of you."

"I think you need to stay in a place and make some friends. You need something to make you happy."

"Look, I have to work that stuff out. That's not something you have to worry about." He stood up and grabbed a shirt off a chair. "Let's go get something to eat. And then we'll go see Arnie. We missed your appointment yesterday, but maybe he'll work us in anyway."

"I need to go back and see Melissa. I shouldn't have left the way I did."

"You're right about that. The poor girl has been crying her eyes out. She's called me four times."

David had thought that would be the case and he was sorry.

"I'll tell you what. I'll call her. Maybe she can meet us somewhere, and we'll all have lunch together. I'll call Arnie and see if he can work us in this afternoon. Okay?"

"Okay."

"That's good. I feel good about that. Don't you?" Paul smiled—showed that movie star smile of his. But it didn't look real.

17

Paul and David were sitting in a booth in a little downtown restaurant. It was an old place, and it was sort of run-down. But Paul said the food was good. David was drinking a Pepsi and Paul a cup of coffee. They were waiting for Melissa before they ordered lunch.

"Where are you going to go, Paul?" David asked.

"When? After I leave the Jefferson?"

"Yeah."

"I don't know. I don't know too many people around here. I guess I'll check with the union and check with the hotels here in town. Maybe. Or maybe I'll just head for San Francisco."

"I thought you wanted to stay away from there." David sucked on the straw in his drink. He was watching Paul, trying to decide what Paul was feeling now.

"Yeah. Well, I don't know. One thing I was thinking was that I might try to find my daughters. Last I knew, they were still in California."

"How come you don't know where they are?"

Paul held the coffee in both hands, like a bowl of soup, and he stared into it, not drinking for the moment. "Well, if I were a decent father—a decent man—I would know. But I'm not."

"You're going to try to find them, aren't you?"

"I was thinking about it. But they probably hate me. They may not want to hear from me." He paused and then added, "I've got another daughter somewhere. I think she's in Redwood City, but I'm not sure."

"They probably want to see you."

"I doubt it, David. I know what their mothers have told them about me. And it's all true. Every word."

"Maybe you're different now."

"Maybe."

"My dad wasn't so great, but I still miss him."

Paul looked up. "What do you mean, he wasn't so great?"

"He got mad a lot. And he didn't have much to do with me. He never played with me or anything like that."

"How come you miss him?"

David shrugged. "He was my dad."

Paul nodded, still looking at David. "What about your mom? Was she pretty great?"

"Yeah."

"I take it you didn't have a whole lot. What did your dad do for a living?"

167

"Anything he could. Mostly he was out of work. My mom was a waitress. She worked more than he did."

"But it wasn't so bad, huh?"

"I don't know. I played with my brother. I miss him. Dad was funny sometimes—when he was in a good mood—and Mom talked to me a lot."

"Well, I'll tell you, David, you've been a little short on breaks in your life. You've already gone through more stuff than most kids ever do."

David didn't look at Paul, didn't answer. But it was something he had thought of lots of times. He had watched the movies, seen the families, seen the Christmas mornings with all the presents, seen the summer vacations, the fancy bedrooms.

"I'll tell you something, David. I look at you, and I think, 'How come adults can't handle this whole thing better? How come they don't give a kid like this a better deal?' And then I look at me, and I think what I did myself—what I did to my daughters. I'm the one who caused the mess for those kids. And the trouble is, now there isn't one thing I can do about it."

"You didn't mean to mess up."

"That doesn't make things right. But nothing seems right. All these teachers and parents and everybody are always telling kids how they're supposed to act—and then the adults don't act right themselves."

"Just some of them."

"Yeah, I guess. But all I know is that I'm one of the bad ones. My whole life I've been telling myself that I'm somebody, that I've got class—just because I can get two bucks out of a guy most bellboys only get one from. But that doesn't mean anything to me anymore. I'm no better than Ralph."

"You didn't have to do the stuff you did for me."

"Yeah. But I'll tell you why I did it. I looked at you and I saw me. The same thing happened to all of us. I talked to Melissa about it. Most of us at the hotel are people who feel like we're sort of on our own—we didn't want to see a little kid like you already going through the same thing."

David thought about it all for a time. He tried to think what had happened to him. "It's not just parents who mess up," he said. "I messed up, too. I got too mad at Mr. Poulter. I don't blame him for hating me. But at the hotel, nobody would let me hate them."

Melissa finally came in, wearing jeans and a big woolly sweater. She sat next to David, put her arm around him, and pulled him close to her. "You little devil. You scared me to death. Why did you do that?"

Paul helped. He ran down the story for her. "But we've talked it over," Paul said. "He's going to go over to Social Services this afternoon and see what they can work out."

"That's best, David," Melissa said. "You know that. I thought we had that all worked out."

David didn't want to say he had been lying, so he said nothing. Paul waved for the waitress to come over, and the three ordered their lunch. David ordered a hamburger in a basket. It had potato chips, not french fries, and some coleslaw, which he didn't like. Paul ordered David another Pepsi, too.

In a few minutes the three of them were teasing and

laughing, and yet, David knew that the whole thing was forced, that no one really felt that happy. Melissa kept touching David's arm with her elbow. He knew she had no idea how much he liked that.

"Have you been looking around for another job?" Melissa asked Paul.

"Not yet. I've gotta get started."

Melissa nodded, and then she glanced at David. "I might be leaving the hotel, too."

David looked up at her. "Where are you going?"

"I think I might go home."

"Where is that?" Paul asked. "Michigan?"

"Minnesota."

"You told me you wouldn't ever go back there."

"I know. I've said a lot of things." She sipped at her Coke and set it down. "I called my mom last night. It's been so long and I've hurt her so badly, but I can't believe it, she wants me to come back. She says I could live at home and finish my high school work, then go to a college over in the next town. She's willing to try to forget the past."

"Could you live in a little town like that again?"

"I don't know. I've always said I couldn't, but maybe I can. Maybe I can be the homecoming queen, meet some nice college boy, and get married." She laughed.

"I'll bet you do," Paul said.

"Hey, I'm just joking."

"Why?"

"I don't think I have to answer that."

"Melissa, let me tell you something." Paul was holding a steak sandwich. He set it down and wiped some juice from his hand with the little paper napkin he had never put in his lap. "You're a beautiful woman. And a good one. Those kids coming out of high school may be too young for you, but you'll run into some older guys—maybe guys who've worked a little and are going back to school. You'll probably marry one of those guys and end up living in some town out there. It'll be just what you need—just what you want, really."

"Maybe. I don't know."

"I think it is. And it's a lot easier to change when you're your age than it is when you're mine."

After they finished eating, no one left. They sat together, really not saying all that much, but no one seemingly eager to move on. "I guess maybe we ought to head over to Social Services," Paul finally said. "We missed our appointment, but I called Arnie. He said to come over this afternoon and he'll work us in. Melissa, do you want to go with us?"

"No. I guess not. But, David, if they don't get anything worked out today, you can come back tonight. I still have some of your stuff at my house."

"Okay."

"I won't say good-bye. I'm sure I'll see you. At least you'll have to get someone to bring you by to pick up your stuff."

David nodded.

"I'll be right back," Paul said. "I'm going to the men's room."

David thought he was leaving on purpose, which was fine with him. He wanted to say something to Melissa. He doubted he could, but he wanted to.

"David," Melissa said, as soon as Paul walked away, "I was just heartbroken yesterday. I didn't know what to do. I just sat there and cried."

"I'm sorry."

"Where were you going?"

"California."

"You can't do that. You'd never—"

"I know. I won't do it again."

"It hurt me so much, David, and then I thought what I did to my mother when I walked out the way I did. I just hadn't ever realized. That's why I called her. And then she said she wanted me to come home." Melissa's eyes were full of tears. "David, you've been so good for me. I care about you. I hope you won't forget that." She pulled him close.

David tried not to cry, and then he gave up and pushed his head against her shoulder and let himself go. He cried as he hadn't cried in a very long time. She held him close and he sobbed. He was afraid people would see, could hear, but he couldn't hold back any longer.

Melissa kept patting him on the back, saying, "Everything's going to be okay now. We'll make sure you get a nice place to live."

"Melissa," David said, gulping to get his voice under control, "I don't want to lose you forever. . . ." It was too stupid, too embarrassing. He couldn't tell her what he really meant.

But she seemed to understand. "Oh, David," she said. "Oh, David. No one ever said such a lovely thing to me. Not ever." But she couldn't finish either. She clung to

David and sobbed, the tears wetting his hair. And he just kept crying, knowing that she would leave and he would never see her again, no matter what they said now. Nothing ever seemed to work in this world, he told himself. Things just kept going wrong.

18

Paul and David took a taxi to the Social Services office. When they walked inside, Paul told David to sit down in a waiting area, and then he went over and talked to a receptionist. He came back and said, "Arnie has someone in his office for a few minutes." He sat down and picked up a magazine from a coffee table, and he began to thumb through it.

David was nervous. He had finally admitted to himself that he was going to have to try another family. But he didn't want to think about it. Every time the thought came to him, he remembered Mr. Poulter and the homes he had been in before.

Arnie came out after ten minutes or so. He was a young guy, but his hair was receding a little and he wore wire-rim glasses that looked like the ones in World War II movies. He said, "Hi, David." He sounded gentle.

The three of them walked back to Arnie's office together. Arnie pulled a chair out from behind the desk, and he sat close to Paul and David, facing them. Paul explained what had happened. "Look, Arnie," he said. "David and I had a pretty good talk this morning. He's still not too excited about going into another home, but then, he's had some pretty bad experiences already. Since his parents got in that wreck, he's been passed around a lot. From what he said about the families he's been with, I wouldn't want to live with them either."

"David, where did you live when you were with your parents?" Arnie asked. He pushed his glasses up with one finger.

"We lived in a trailer, and we moved quite a bit. My dad would move when he could find a job. I was born in Bellingham, and we lived up around there until I was eight, and then we moved to Everett."

"And that's where you were living when the accident happened?"

David nodded.

"What's your last name?"

David took a breath.

"Look, Arnie, he's not too sure he wants to go through with this," Paul said. "I told him to listen to you and find out what you could do for him, and then he could decide."

Arnie said, "Okay," and nodded a couple of times, but he looked at David and said, "What will you do if you don't like what I have to say?" He smiled.

"I don't know."

"Well, that's just it. I'm really sorry you were placed

with families you didn't like very much. But, David, this sort of thing isn't easy. If you can live with a nice, stable family, people who will take good care of you and make sure you get an education, you're going to be a—"

"Come on, Arnie," Paul said. "The kid doesn't need a 'nice, stable family.' He needs someone who'll treat him like they maybe like him. He was stuck with some lady this last time who was scared he might get a little mud on her floors and a man who told him no one was ever going to like him. What he needs this time is someone who loves him."

"I know," Arnie said. "We'll do our best to get him a good situation this time. Mostly, with older children, we have to look to foster parents. Some of them take in two or three kids at a time, maybe more. Most of them are really good and really take good care of the kids. But there aren't all that many who want to do it. We get some couples who are a little older, who decide they want to try an older child—maybe they haven't had kids, and they don't want to start with a baby—but often they don't like to commit to anything long term until they've gotten to know the child."

"That's what he got into this last time."

Arnie nodded. "Yes, that's what I assumed. And maybe they were a little stiff. This time might be a lot better."

"But when I talked to you, you said you were sure you could find him a nice family."

"We will, Paul. I'm sure we will. But I can't guarantee anything overnight. It might take—"

"Where's David going to sleep tonight then? What happens to him while you're trying to figure something out?"

"We'll work something out. I'll have to make some calls. We have certain families who'll take a child on a temporary basis. At worst, we might have to put him in an institutional setting for a few nights. But at least he won't be out in the streets. Anything is better than that."

"What do you mean—institutional? Is that some kind of detention center?"

"Well, Paul, what do you expect?" Arnie took his glasses off and wiped the side of his nose with his finger tips. "The first thing we have to do is find him a warm place to sleep, where he'll be fed and taken care of. That will be with a family, if at all possible. Getting the right sort of family might take a little time."

"Arnie, this kid has been through too much of that kind of crap already. He needs to get settled in with someone who'll give him a real home."

"Paul, I can't just snap my fingers and make that happen by magic. There's some red tape we have to take care of, for one thing. He was with a family, and I guess the Everett office handled it. We may have to transfer the paperwork or maybe send him up there. Things like that take a little while. We'll try not to move him around a lot, but I can't promise a permanent home right away."

Paul swore. "That's not what you said on the phone. You made it sound like you could work things out without any trouble."

Arnie raised his hands in frustration. "Look, Paul, we were talking about getting a kid off the streets. I can do that. I know the rest of the process is not ideal. But I can't bring David's parents back. I can't go to the door and call out for two lovely parents to come up and take David off to a perfect home full of warmth and love and everything else he needs. I wish I could."

"You people here had two years, Arnie. Two years. And this kid's been kicked around until he decided he'd rather live in the streets."

Arnie started to answer, and then he simply let his breath escape. "I know. I'm sorry. But I don't know what else to do but keep trying."

David was looking at the floor, the hard brown carpet. He wished he could find some of the anger again, but now he was only feeling that he was glad that he hadn't come with great hopes.

"Can I adopt him?" Paul asked.

David looked up.

But Arnie was shaking his head. "Paul, come on. You know better."

"Why? Because I'm not married, or because I'm a drunk, or because I'm a bellboy, or what?"

"Being single doesn't rule you out, but your background would. You've had a drinking problem; you've moved around a lot. You told me yourself that you didn't send child support to your own children."

David watched Paul, saw his frustration, his controlled anger. "And it doesn't matter that I happen to care about this kid?"

"Sure, that's important. But what do you expect us to do? We try to get him the kind of stable family that will provide for him best. What if the state gave him to you, and then you started to drink again? People would say we just dumped him off on someone. We have to consider things like that."

"Maybe if I had David I wouldn't drink anymore. I'm trying to change, Arnie, but I need—you know—something to live for."

"That all sounds good, Paul. But how do you know you wouldn't get frustrated after a while. David's about to be a teenager. It's not easy to raise teenagers."

"So he goes to a temporary home—or maybe a detention center—for a week or two, or maybe longer. By then you try to find him a permanent family—which aren't that easy to find. And so he just might get kicked around for months or years again. And that's better than taking a chance on me?"

"I don't know whether it's better, Paul. It depends on how things work out. But it's the only way we can do it."

Paul put his head down, held his forehead with both hands. He stayed that way for a very long time. Arnie seemed to be thinking, too. Finally Paul looked up and said, "Arnie, for a week I've been promising this boy that if we came down here, you could work things out for him. And every time he has told me he wouldn't come because he knew you couldn't do anything. I didn't understand that. I couldn't figure how a little kid could already be so negative about everything in his life. Now I know why."

Arnie looked back at Paul for quite some time, and then he leaned back in his chair and looked beyond Paul. "Okay, listen," he eventually said, and shook his head. "I could possibly let you be a temporary foster parent. I could start looking for a permanent family for him, but in the meantime, you could keep him with you. I can't even talk with you about adoption, but I have a lot more leeway with foster homes. If I reported everything I know about you, I'd get the papers kicked right back in my face. But I won't do that."

Paul stood up. "Okay. What do we do?" David was stunned. This all seemed impossible.

"Just sit down." Arnie opened a desk drawer and got out some papers. And then he stopped and looked at David. "We haven't asked you. Do you want to live with Paul?"

"Yes."

"Okay. But I want you to call me if Paul ever has a drink. Will you do that?"

David nodded, and Arnie looked back at Paul. "Are you still living downtown in that hotel?"

"Yeah. But I'm planning on moving right away."

"Okay. I'll hold the papers for a few days. We won't put down an address until you get something better. Where can he stay tonight?"

"With Melissa."

Arnie looked a little worried about that. He thought it over for several seconds, then said, "Okay. But let's pretend you didn't even come here today. We'll start this whole thing when you've moved. At least I can show that you've got a stable job. How long have you been at the Jefferson?"

Paul looked over at David. He seemed to hold his breath for a time and then let go. "About a year. And I'm planning to stay on there." He nodded to David, affirming that he meant it.

David knew what the words had cost him. He could hardly believe it.

"Paul, this whole thing is strictly temporary. But you could end up having him quite a while. I'm not sure you know what you're getting yourself into."

"Yeah, I think I do. I want to do it. This isn't just off the top of my head. I've been thinking about it for a few days."

"You've got to prove yourself—show me you can handle this. You've got to find a decent neighborhood and get him in school. What will you do if he has trouble with his schoolwork? Can you help him at all?"

Paul shrugged. "Not that much. I can try." He looked down for a moment. "But I know some people who'll be glad to help. Melissa, at least for now. And Rob—you know, the night auditor. He's had some college. Maybe I can try to find an apartment close to where he lives on Capitol Hill. Melissa's in that area, too. They can come over sometimes and help out. Betty would help, too."

"Maybe. But people are busy, and they—"

"No. They like David. They'd want to help."

"All right." Arnie was looking at the papers, or maybe just the desk. He sat for some time. "Paul, I sure hope I'm doing the right thing. I've never gone out on a limb like this before. If you mess up, I'm going to be responsible."

"Don't worry."

Arnie nodded. "Okay. We'll try it. Go ahead now. Come back when you've got an address you can give me.

We'll have to fill out a number of forms. Call me if there's a problem of any kind."

Paul stood up. "Arnie, don't worry. I'm going to do things right this time. I'll keep him until you're really sure you've got just the right family for him." He put his hand on David's back, and David felt the softness of his touch this time. They walked out the door and on out of the building. Outside, Paul kept going, turning right and walking down the sidewalk.

"Where are we going?" David asked.

"I don't know. I haven't thought that far ahead." And then, after walking a little way, he added, "There's a gas station a couple of blocks down. Let's walk over there and call Melissa. Maybe she can come and get you. I've got to go down to the hotel."

"Are you going to talk to Ralph?"

"Yeah."

"Can you do it?"

"I'll do it." He nodded resolutely. "I've done worse things. Are you really sure you want to live with me?"

"Yeah. I do."

"Okay." He was walking rather fast. A light rain was falling, and the sky was a layer of lead-gray clouds. It was probably cold, but David didn't feel it. "David, I don't have any idea why you like me, but I guess you do. And I like you. We'll just make the best of things. It isn't like when you had a family, but it's better than what Arnie was talking about."

"We'll be okay," David said.

"You've gotta work hard in school and do better with your reading."

"I will. I'll practice every day."

"Yeah, that's right. I'll only give you one hour of TV."

He laughed.

"That's okay."

Paul stopped and looked down at David. "It isn't going to be that great, David. No matter how you look at it, this just isn't what you deserve. I hope everyone will help, like I said they would. I think they will. And then I hope Arnie can find you a really great family who'll adopt you—and, you know, do the whole thing right."

"Maybe you could marry Melissa. Then you could adopt me."

Paul shook his head slowly and said "That's not going to happen either, David. I think you know that. This isn't the movies—or some fairy tale. There's no way things are going to be what we wish they would be. But I . . . really like you. You know what I mean? So I'll do the best I can."

David nodded, and he said to himself, "We'll be all right." He thought of stepping closer to Paul, but he didn't do it. The two of them started walking again. He slid his hand into his pocket and felt the knife, and he thought of Billy, and then his mother—as a sort of test. The pain was still there; the memory hadn't changed. But he hadn't expected that it would.

David realized he was scared, still careful about getting too excited about anything. Too many things had gone wrong before. He didn't expect the sun to come out all of a sudden, and the air to get warm and the birds to start singing—the way it happened in the movies. He knew better than that. He didn't even expect the rain to stop.

But something felt right. He had friends—almost a family. He had felt like a stranger for so long, and now he felt like David again. He hadn't felt that way since that day on the freeway, just before the car started to skid.